SAVAGE SPADES

K.D Clark

Copy Editor: Underline This Editing
https://www.underlinethisediting.net/

Beta Reader: EditForContent
https://www.editforcontent.com/beta-reading

First paperback edition February 2020

Visit my website: https://kdclark.blog/

Also by K. D. Clark

The New York Capos Series

Merciless Queen

Twisted Judgement

Fallen Judgement

Apprehension

Admission

CHAPTER ONE

Kit

"Fuck, are you sure it was Dustin?" he asked.

Gunner, the club president, nodded. "The girl remembers everything. Says that Dustin took her out to the woods and raped her."

"That sick son of a bitch," said Zeke, the Vice President, as he shook his head.

They sat around the large table in the meeting room down the hall from the bar. It's where they came to discuss things that were going on in their town as well as club business.

"What about the cops? Shouldn't they be throwing his ass in a cement cell?" Zeke asked.

"He posted bail. Sheriff Garrett said they couldn't keep him," Gunner replied.

Zeke's hands formed into fists on top of the wooden table they all sat at.

"So what's the plan?" Kit asked.

Women didn't get hurt or raped in their town without someone paying for it. They were all at different levels of pissed off but Zeke especially since he had a little girl at home.

"I say we burn the place to the fucking ground," Zeke said. "That's what the sick bastard deserves."

"We've been going to Old Timers for years. Isn't there something else we can do instead of burning it to the ground?" Jett, the Road Captain, asked.

"He's a fucking rapist. Even if we didn't burn the place to the ground, you think we'd go back there?" Zeke snapped.

Gunner sat back in his chair and ran a hand over his bald head. They were all dressed in their leather cuts. It was a jacket with the sleeves cut off and the club name sewed on the back in big orange letters: Savage Spades. Anytime they had to come together, either for a meeting or a ride, they were required to wear the cut. Most of them wore it nearly every day. It was an honor to have the cut and everyone in this room had worked their ass off to get it.

"I'm just saying, we could just beat the shit out of him then leave the bar," Jett argued.

Zeke was already shaking his head. "Nah, brother, nothing is going to hurt him more than watching that precious bar burn to the ground. We got to burn it."

Zeke looked around the table. Kit nodded his support. He agreed with Zeke completely; the bar needed to go. He'd miss all the time they'd spent there over the years, but Dustin was a sick bastard and they had to put him out of business one way or another. The other men around the table nodded their agreement as well.

Gunner sat up in the chair and grabbed the gavel. "Then it's settled. We'll ride at midnight."

"Midnight? It's going to be packed," Kit said.

Gunner turned and smiled at him. "I think we should make a bit of a show, huh?"

Gunner slammed the gavel on the table, signally Church was over. Kit stood up with the rest of the men and walked out of the meeting room to the bar area. Jett landed a smack on his shoulder as he walked down the hallway.

"You ready for this?" Jett asked.

"Fuck yeah, it's been too quiet around here."

Jett laughed. Anytime they went for a ride, he was the one that planned and made sure they didn't run into any trouble. Unlike most of the guys in the club, Jett had a slender build. He wasn't as tall as Kit but he came close at six foot. His beard was patchy at best but Jett didn't seem to care. Compared to Kit the guy was a twig. He was also probably the smartest out of all of them. He's the only brother that'd gone off to college and had a degree to show for it. The rest of them were either felons or veterans. Kit was neither; but when he found the club, he was on his way to being a felon.

"I heard you took two girls back to your room last night," Jett said.

Kit smiled at him and shrugged. "Maybe." Jett laughed again and took a seat on one of the barstools. He'd probably be there for an hour or so, planning out their ride tonight. Goldbeach, North

Carolina had a small population of people, but there was a ton of land to cover. Even though Dustin's bar wasn't very far, Jett knew which way to take to avoid the cops.

He turned away from Jett and looked out at the seating area of the clubhouse. Four girls in cut-off jeans and tight shirts sat at a high table. He was always surprised by their commitment. They were always there, hoping that one of the guys would make them an Old Lady--a woman who is dating or married to one of the members. An Old Lady was held with the most respect and had the protection of the club. Little did these women know, there was no chance in hell they were becoming someone's Old Lady. Most of the guys had no desire to settle down. Like Kit, they just wanted a night of fun. He continued around the bar to the second hallway that led back to some of the rooms. The clubhouse had more rooms than he could count.

There was a room for all of the men as well as anyone that might need a place to stay for the night. The first floor, on the same level as the bar, held five bedrooms--one of them belonged to Gunner. But Gunner rarely used it since he had an Old Lady at home that would probably shoot him in the balls if he didn't come home to her every night.On the lower level was Kit's room. He took the stairs, the sound of his feet echoing off each wooden step. The lower level looked a lot like a basement with a concrete floor and a paneled ceiling. But the rooms down here were just as nice as the ones upstairs. They each even had a bathroom attached. He walked through the first door. The two women from last night were still sleeping on his mattress, completely naked. One blonde; one brunette. He was so drunk last night he'd barely remembered taking them down to his room. He closed the door and kicked the side of the mattress. The blonde jumped awake and glared at him.

"Time to go, sweetheart," he said.

"Why do you always do that, Kit? You can't just let me sleep a bit longer?" she asked.

Warning bells went off in his head. If she'd noticed a pattern, that meant he'd slept with her too many times. He made a mental note to avoid the blonde tonight.

"Can't have you stealin' any of my shit," he said as he crossed the room and started picking up their clothes from the floor. He threw the clothes on the bed and the blonde grabbed them and started to dress. She paused to wake up her friend, and he waited for them to leave. The brunette reached her hand out and rubbed it over the tattoos that covered his left arm on her way out.

"You sure you don't need any help this morning?" she asked in a sultry tone.

His dick twitched at her offer but he had work to take care of. "Maybe another time sweetheart."

She dropped her hand, and he smacked her

ass as she walked past him. Locking the door behind them, he then stripped off his clothes to get into the shower to wash off the smell of booze and sex. He'd usually sleep in longer but with Church this morning, he didn't wanna fall back asleep.

After taking a quick shower, he walked to the back of the clubhouse where his garage was. When he'd wanted to open a repair shop, Gunner had offered to have it built on the land next to the clubhouse. It'd worked out perfectly for Kit since he was only steps away from his job, and he was able to hire his brothers. When he entered, he was surprised to see Hugo there, working on a Mercedes. Kit slapped his hand.

"Couldn't sleep either?" Hugo asked.

Hugo was the only brother that was bigger than Kit. He stood a few inches taller and could almost double Kit's bench press. Hugo's beard was full and he didn't have tattoos on his arm like Kit did.

Kit shrugged. "Figure I'd get to work."

Hugo used the wrench to point over to a bike in the corner.

"Gunner needs an oil change if you wanna get started on that."

Kit nodded and made his way over to the bike.

*****

"We need to make sure everyone is out of the bar before we light it up. Got it?" Gunner yelled, over the sound of all their engines. Kit bounced his knee against the bike, ready to start the ride.

They all nodded their heads in understanding. Jett took off first, next was Gunner, Zeke, and then the rest of them. It was a warm night so he didn't wear anything under his cut beside a thin, gray t-shirt. The wind rippled through his shirt as the bike bumped over the dirt roads until they made it out of the clubhouse to the smooth pavement. They rode faster than the speed limit, passing other cars and probably scaring the shit out of the drivers. There was no greater high than riding, especially on a warm night like tonight. Riding is what brought them all together. It was the entire point of the Savage Spades.

When he was a teenager, filled with anger and nowhere to let it out, he'd take his bike on the road just like this. Nothing else calmed him down like riding. The family that came with being a member of the club was just a side effect. Riding in a group this large required a great deal of trust. It was why they referred to each other as brothers. They were more than just a group of men who spent time together...they were a brotherhood.

The ride ended too soon. They stopped in front of Old Timers. The big, neon 'open' sign hung over the wooden porch. A few people stood outside with beer bottles in their hands but judging by the number of cars in the gravel parking lot, there were a lot more inside. It was the usual bar they frequented so no one would even raise an eyebrow to all the bikes showing upfront. If anything, Dustin was probably restocking the keg right now to get ready for them. Kit shut the engine off and climbed off his bike, setting the helmet on the back.

"Hugo, I need you to get all the innocents out first. Ace, make sure Dustin doesn't try to run," Gunner said.

Hugo went into the bar first, and Ace walked around the back. It wasn't long before people started rushing out the front door. When a man the size of Hugo tells you to do something, people usually listen. Women in cut-off shorts and cowboy boots dashed to their cars already knowing that something bad was going to happen. Most people would consider it a risk to hang out at Old Timers anyways since everyone in town knew that's where the Savage Spades liked to spend their time.

Once almost all the cars in the parking lot were gone, Gunner walked inside. Zeke followed behind him, and Kit followed afterward. Ace was sitting across the bar from Dustin with a hard look in his eyes. Dustin's eyes were wide and a bead of sweat ran from his forehead down to his chin. Hugo stood at the back exit with his arms crossed over his chest, like some kind of bouncer.

"Everyone get out?" Gunner asked Hugo.

"All clear, just this piece of shit."

The front door slammed and they all turned their heads to see Jett dragging in a canister of gasoline. Dustin tried to take advantage of the distraction and run from behind the bar, but Ace was out of the barstool in a flash. He shoved Dustin so he fell on the sticky floor.

"Listen, I don't know what you think I did, but don't do this," Dustin begged as he pushed himself across the floor, trying to get away from them. He had nowhere to go.

"We don't give mercy to a rapist," Zeke spat, his eyes holding a kind of rage that Kit had never seen before.

Dustin's eyes widened. "Rapist?"

Zeke grabbed the gun from his waistband and slapped Dustin across the face with it. Once, then twice. Gunner grabbed Zeke's arm before he could hit him a third time.

"Tie him up," Gunner told Hugo.

"Come on, Gunner! I didn't do it! I would never do that," Dustin pleaded, his face covered with blood and tears.

"Shut up!" Gunner barked.

Dustin fought and screamed as Hugo grabbed the rope and tied Dustin's feet and hands together like a pig ready to be roasted.

"Burn in hell," Zeke said before aiming the gun at Dustin's head and pulling the trigger.

The noise echoed off the walls and it took a minute for Kit to be able to hear again. He turned his head away not, wanting to see the lifeless body.

"Jett, light it up," Gunner said before walking out of the bar.

They all followed behind Gunner while Jett spilled the gasoline everywhere.Kit got on his bike and watched as the bar slowly started to go up in flames. Jett ran out of the bar just in time to get on his bike and watch the show with everyone else.

"I guess we're going to need to find a new place to drink," Jett said.

CHAPTER TWO

Cam

The heavy, wooden door creaked as she opened it. The room was pitch black, and it took a few stutters for the overhead lights to illuminate the space once she'd flipped the switch. With the room fully lit, she let the door close behind her before walking toward the bar. The smell of smoke and whiskey lingered in the air. To most people, it might be off-putting, but for Cam, it was a comforting scent. A reminder of her father.

Her flip-flops padded against the wood floor as she maneuvered her way around the tables. The seat of the chairs lay across the tabletop, just the way she'd left them the night before. She pulled a glass from one of the shelves behind the bar and poured some water. She'd done this routine so many times it was ingrained in her brain. She could open and close the bar with her eyes closed at this point. Lifting the glass to her lips, she gulped down the cool water.

She looked up at the clock hanging above the liquor shelf. Two p.m. One hour until Ernie, one of her regulars, would be walking through the door asking for a shot of whiskey and a beer to wash it down. Ernie could drink a scary combination of alcohol and still walk out of here completely fine.

She set the glass of water down and went back out to the floor to start pulling the chairs from the tables. A year ago, her father would have been sitting in the back office, starting on morning paperwork while she opened the bar. But she couldn't let her mind go there today. Any minute now, Jen and Amire would be walking in to start their shift, and if she had a bad attitude, it would affect the entire atmosphere.

Today's going to be a busy day. Maybe if she kept telling herself that, then the man in the sky would listen and send some customers her way. God knew she needed them. You'd think in such a small town, with a limited number of bars, she'd be packed every night. Instead, she was lucky to get a few new customers a week. At this point, Ernie was keeping the lights on.

As she set the last chair down, the front door opened, and Amire walked in.

"Fuck, it's hot outside," he said, repeating her steps and going behind the bar to get a glass of water.

"Said it's supposed to be in the hundreds all week," she said, putting on a smile and pulling herself up to sit on the bar.

Amire raised an eyebrow at her. "What do you want, Cam?"

He always knew when she was up to no

good. He gulped down the water, his Adam's apple bobbing underneath his dark skin.

"Make me some chicken fingers before we open?" she asked, batting her eyelashes. Her stomach had been rumbling since the moment she'd woken up, but the only thing in her fridge was old leftovers from Helen's Diner.

He rolled his eyes before setting the glass down and used the rubber band around his wrist to pull his long dreads into a loose, low ponytail. "What time did you go to sleep?"

She shrugged. "I closed last night, and then I went out with Jen. Well, we stayed in, then we went back to our place."

Amire shook his head. "I can't keep up with you two."

She laughed. "I know. That's why you went home right after your shift. You could have had a couple drinks with us."

Amire never hung out with them after work no matter how many times they invited him. He grabbed a white towel from one of the shelves underneath the counter and threw it over his shoulder.

"No, thank you. I like to be awake with the rest of the world. At least for a little while. You know, if you had a man at home, you'd have a reason to want to crawl in bed after your shift."

She let out a short laugh. "He would be the most neglected man in the world. I have too much going on right now to worry about someone else."

It had been too long since she had even thought about dating someone. She barely noticed the guys in town or anyone in her classes. They all looked the same to her, not interesting enough to break through her tunnel vision.

Amire scoffed. She waved a hand at him, and he turned to go towards the kitchen.

The kitchen prep was simple since they only sold typical bar food. At one point or another, she'd worked every position. When she'd moved across the country from Seattle, Washington to Goldbeach, North Carolina, she knew she'd end up working at her dad's bar. What she hadn't realized was that she would be running it years later.

She walked to the back office. A small space, maybe the size of a large closet at best. The only thing in the office was her desk and a coat rack for Jen and Amire to use. Four, large stacks of papers covered the small desk. She needed to get a filing cabinet to organize all the paperwork but that was going to have to wait.

She slid the first stack of paperwork towards her. Invoices. Some paid; some overdue. The bills never stopped, and sadly, there wasn't enough coming in to take care of them all. She pulled out the five, unpaid invoices from the pile and organized them by priority. Grabbing the checkbook off the desk, she wrote a check for the electric bill, her liquor distributor, and the plumber who fixed the backed-up toilet a couple of weeks ago.

The other two would have to wait until she had more money. She didn't even want to think about the debt that she owed beyond these small invoices. Notably, the most significant debt that her dad left to her. The money should have never been borrowed in the first place. It sent chills down her spine and made her palms sweaty just from thinking about it. Taking a deep breath, she ran her hands over her face, trying to clear her mind. Focus on one thing at a time. Her priority was always to make sure Amire and Jen got paid on time. Even though most bartenders worked solely off tips, she paid Jen an hourly, living wage to make up for the lack of tipping customers. And since she and Jen lived together, it would be an awkward conversation if Jen didn't make enough to pay her half of the bills.

Setting the two, unpaid invoices to the side, she grabbed the next pile of paperwork.

Twenty minutes later, the sound of the front door shutting brought her attention back to the bar. She walked out of the office just as Jen walked around the counter with a cup carrier filled with big, styrofoam cups.

"You are a lifesaver," Cam said as Jen set the cup holder down on the bar. Cam took one of the cups and stuck a straw inside. She loved the way the bubbles from the soda gave that slight burn to the back of her throat. Drinking so much soda was probably the reason her jeans were starting to get tight again, but she didn't care about her weight anymore. She accepted the fact that her body was made different from someone like Jen. Whereas she and Jen could eat the same thing, Cam would always have a more curvy shape. Plus, she'd given up on diets a long time ago. She realized her brain power could be used in better ways other than worrying about a little extra fat.

"No problem, I figured we might need some caffeine," Jen said.

They had soda at the bar, but the gas station down the street must have done something special because it tasted so much better. Of course, she'd never tell her customers that.

"Amire! I brought soda!" Jen yelled. She was a small person but had the voice of an opera singer.

"I can hear you, Jen, you don't have to yell," he complained from the kitchen that was straight to the left of the bar.

Jen winked at her and went to give the soda to Amire. Cam leaned against the counter and sipped on her drink. They had thirty minutes until the bar opened, and she prayed it would be a busy night.

CHAPTER THREE

Cam

Beep. Beep. Beep.

"Turn it off!" Jen yelled from the other room.

Cam had been listening to the alarm for a while but was too tired to turn it off. With a sigh, she cracked open one eye and grabbed the phone off the bedside table before swiping to turn it off.

The summer heat clung to her skin like a pair of tight jeans. The only thing keeping her mildly cool was the box fan she had set up in the corner. The air conditioner had gone out two weeks ago, and the landlord had yet to fix it.

She laid on her back and rubbed a hand over her face. She needed to get ready to meet with her advisor on campus. As soon as she'd moved to Goldbeach, she'd applied to go to the local community college to study graphic design. Today, she needed to register for her classes before all the good ones were taken.

She could only take classes during the day so that she could run the bar at night, but she couldn't take them too early or else she'd never get any sleep. She counted to three and then sat up.

Less than fifteen minutes to get her ass dressed and down to the college.

She shouldn't have drunk so much last night, but Jen was a bad influence. Plus, there were only a couple more weeks until she'd be too busy to have any fun. Her head spun a bit as she crossed the room and went into the small, shared bathroom located in the hallway between the bedrooms. They lived in a small house, which meant there was very little privacy. Hence, why Jen could hear Cam's alarm from her bedroom. It was even worse when Jen brought a guy home. On those nights, Cam had to plug in her earbuds and turn up the volume to drown out the sound of Jen's moans.

She stripped off her clothes and turned the shower on. It took a minute for the water to make its way through the pipes to the shower head. It took even longer for the water to heat up enough for her to get in. She washed away the smell of sweat and alcohol with her strawberry-scented body wash before brushing her teeth in the shower to save on time.

Once she stepped out of the shower, she wrapped a white towel around her body before running a brush through her wet hair and throwing it up in a bun. In her bedroom, she changed into a white, spaghetti strap top and a pair of jean shorts before slipping her feet into her pink flip-flops. The time on her phone told her she still had ten minutes left before she had to get out the door.

Just enough time to make some coffee.

Feeling more awake than she had moments ago, she walked to the kitchen. Jen was scheduled to open the bar today, so that gave Cam some free time after she got done signing up for classes. That meant she could run to the store and pick up some stuff they needed for the house. She'd also been needing to do her laundry since she was running very low on clothes. If she didn't do laundry today, she'd be wearing swimsuit bottoms as underwear tomorrow. She filled the coffee maker with the coffee grounds and water and leaned against the counter, waiting for it to brew. Even when she had 'free' time, she spent it catching up on all the things she'd been putting off. She wished that time would slow down so she could catch her breath.

Jen walked in, dressed in a pair of pajama pants and a tank top. Her bright, red hair was tousled and wild.

"Hey, sunshine," Cam greeted, plastering a smile on her face to hopefully make up for the fact that her alarm woke Jen up.

"Someone's peachy this morning."

Cam shrugged. "I will be once I get some coffee in me."

Jen pulled out one of the falling-apart wooden chairs from the table and plopped down.

"What are your plans?" she asked Jen before grabbing a to-go coffee mug from the cabinet and started to fill it up.

"Get my shit back from Jason," Jen said.

"He still hasn't dropped it off?"

Jen was a serial dater. She didn't usually keep a boyfriend for longer than a couple of months.

Jen let out an annoyed breath. "No, I'm sure he wants me to come over so he can try to apologize for cheating on me."

Cam placed the lid on her coffee cup. "What a tool."

"Aren't they all?" Jen asked, and her eyes held a sadness behind them as she looked at Cam.

Cam felt terrible for Jen. She wore her heart on her sleeve and fell in love fast, usually with the wrong type of guy. "I'm sorry," she said.

Jen gave her a sad smile. "Another one bites the dust."

Cam threw her purse over her shoulder. "I'll see you tonight? Don't forget you're opening."

"Yep, see you tonight," Jen said as Cam left and got into her pick up truck.

The big, blue truck was old, and she had to jump to get in, but her father left it to her, and she didn't have the money to buy anything else. After a while, she'd gotten used to Big Blue. It never gave her any trouble despite how old it was. She made a mental note to get an oil change. It had to be past due.

The drive to the local college was short. She could walk if she had to. If she didn't have Big Blue, that would be her only option since there wasn't any public transportation in Goldbeach. There weren't any bus stops until you got closer to the Charlotte. It was completely different from Seattle where everything was convenient. Small things like that made her miss living in a big city, but there was nothing for her in Seattle anymore. She parked in a spot up front and got to her advisor's office just in time.

"Ms. Hamilton, it's nice to see you," Mr. Jones said as Cam sat down in the chair across from him.

"Nice to see you too," she said.

He looked more like an athletic coach than he did an academic advisor with short, military-cut hair and broad shoulders. His graying hair and pictures of his teenage children around the office gave away his age, but if she had to guess, he probably played football in college. She'd gotten to know Mr. Jones well over the last couple semesters. He was also the Digital Photography professor. The college was so small, all the advisors were also professors.

He stared at the computer screen, not saying anything as he clicked his mouse. After a moment, he looked up at her.

"Alright, it looks like you have a while to go before your degree is finished. I see that you didn't pass Algebra last semester. Do you want to try that one again?" he asked.

"Can I take it in the spring?" She'd failed once she didn't want to fail twice in a row.

"Yes, that's fine. What were you thinking for this semester? Are you going full- or part-time?"

Full-time would get her through school faster. She didn't want to be in school until she was fifty, but with running the bar, a full course load wasn't an option.

"Part-time," she said to Mr. Jones.

He gave her a look that was a mix of pity and disappointment. She couldn't blame him. Mr. Jones had been rooting for her since the first day she'd enrolled. He'd seen her struggle to keep up with her courses last semester and skipped classes because she was too tired from staying at the bar the night before. This semester was going to be different. She had to focus on school. She didn't know what the rest of life had in store for her, but she needed this degree as a backup plan.

"There are a couple of visual arts classes you need to take and a history class. Does that work for you? Three classes?" he asked, looking up from the computer.

"What time?"

"One is at nine a.m.; the other two start at eleven a.m., twice a week."

Nine o'clock was early, but she could swing it. She just had to make sure she was out of the bar early the night before.

"I can do it."

"Okay, I'll get your schedule together and send it over."

"Great," she said, getting ready to leave the

office.

"Hey, Cameron," he said, stopping her in her tracks.

She slid back down in the chair.

Mr. Jones readjusted his tie. "I know last semester was really hard for you, and the college has tons of resources if you need help...but because of your grades, you have been put on academic probation."

"What?!" When had this happened? Why didn't anyone tell her?

"You should have gotten a letter sent to your home over the summer."

There was a massive pile of mail sitting on her coffee table at home that she'd barely glanced at.

"What does this mean?"

"It's temporary. If you can get your GPA up this semester, you'll be taken off probation. If not, you could be dismissed."

She ran a hand through her hair. "Great."

This was precisely what she needed: more pressure. In addition to worrying about the bar losing money, she had to worry about possibly getting kicked out of school.

"I know this can be stressful, but we have a lot of tutors--"

"Thank you, Mr. Jones," she said before getting out of the chair and leaving the building. She barely had time to go to school, let alone take advantage of the college's tutoring services. She got into her truck and leaned her head against the hot steering wheel. Life just kept getting better.

*****

The minute the bar came into view, her mouth dropped open. The parking lot was filled with black motorcycles. Usually, she'd be happy for a busy night filled with paying customers, but with the day she had, she'd been looking forward to a quiet night. Since there wasn't anywhere to park in the small lot, she found a spot in front of Ms. Rogers' bookstore. Local, small businesses surrounded the street her bar was on. The strip was usually deserted by 6 p.m. The only places that stayed open late was her bar and Helen's Diner.

The sound of rock music cut through the warm air and filled the cab of her truck. That was unusual. Their regulars liked to watch the game, and most of them could care less about the restored jukebox. She turned off the truck, not bothering to lock the doors before walking across the street. She'd chosen to wear cut-off shorts because it was so hot, but she regretted it now as her thighs rubbed together. The music was so loud she couldn't hear the door creak as she opened it.

She didn't see Ernie sitting on his usual barstool; in his place was a large man the size of a football player. Leather material spread across the man's broad back with the words 'Savage Spades' written in bright orange letters above a picture of a spades card. Looking around the room, she realized everyone in her bar had the same, sleeveless leather jacket on. Most of the men had long beards. Some looked old enough to be her grandfather, while others looked like they were barely out of high school. An older man with a graying beard laughed and sloshed beer onto the table as he slammed the mug down. Some of the men were nursing their drinks while they casually talked. The loud music wasn't doing much to help her headache that had started not long after leaving Mr. Jone's office.

Taking a deep breath, she maneuvered around the full tables to the bar where Jen was laying out glasses. Some of her red hair stuck to her face with sweat.

"What's going on?" Cam asked.

Jen looked up, as if realizing for the first time that Cam had walked through the door.

"I don't know. They came in a couple of hours ago, all on their motorcycles. Most of the regulars left, but they're ordering a lot and tipping, so I'm happy."

Jen grabbed the ice scoop out of the bucket and filled the glasses before adding a shot of whiskey to each one.

"Can I get another beer?" a guy asked from the end of the bar. His beard was so long it touched his t-shirt. His eyes were slightly glazed over from the alcohol.

"I'll grab these," Cam told Jen as she grabbed the glasses of whiskey, balancing two of them in one hand.

"It's the three men in the corner booth," Jen said.

Cam focused on the glasses, making sure not to tip them over as she walked across the floor. She looked up once she was close to the booth; two of the men were inside the rounded booth while the other had pulled up one of the wooden chairs. They were deep in conversation when she walked up.

"Okay, I got three--"

The man in the chair scooted back, slamming into her stomach. The glasses in her hand smashed into her chest before falling on the ground and shattering. She froze in shock as the cold liquor seeped through her white top, making her bra visible to everyone.

"Ah, shit--"

"Save it," she said through clenched teeth.

She finally looked up at the man responsible for her current situation. Her breath caught in her throat as she was met with baby-blue eyes. They reminded her of the sky on a clear day. His muscular arms were covered in tattoos: a snake, a skull, a few tribal designs, and some other things she couldn't make out. If it was under different circumstances, she might consider him attractive. She looked back up at his face. His eyes were wide and focused on her. They weren't glazed over or red as she expected from a man that'd been drinking for the last couple hours.

Her body was on fire, and she closed her eyes

for a moment, trying to compose herself. When she opened them again, all three men were staring at her like she'd lost her mind. Turning on her heels, she walked out of the bar, grabbing a handful of napkins on the way.

The hot air hit her in the face. She stepped away from the door before leaning against the brick wall next to it. The noise quieted as the door shut. She rubbed the napkins against her shirt, trying her best to dry the stain. Her mind replayed what just happened. She was being dramatic by storming out like that. She could have just accepted the man's apology, gotten a new shirt, and cleaned up, but she had too much on her mind to act rationally.

As she tossed the wet napkins in the nearby trash can, she noticed a pack of cigarettes on the brick window ledge. Someone must have left them. She'd given up smoking months ago, but she needed something to calm her nerves before going back inside. Jen needed her tonight. She grabbed the pack of Newports and opened it, relieved to see that a lighter was inside sandwiched between three cigarettes. She pulled one out and brought it to her lips. She cupped her hand to light it and inhaled. Her body instantly relaxed as the nicotine entered her system.

"That shit will kill you."

She jumped at the deep voice. Blue Eyes stood in front of the closed door. His brown hair was tied up in a bun at the back of his head. Usually, she wasn't a fan of the man-bun trend, but on this guy, it added to his look. His beard was cut short, but it was still very full. She hadn't even heard the door open. Fuck, he had said something to her.

"It's a cigarette, not a bomb," she said, taking another puff. Couldn't she just have a minute of quiet?

"Might as well be," he grumbled.

She caught a glimpse of something silver in his mouth as he spoke. A tongue ring? Really?

"What do you want? Come out here to with your gang spill more whiskey on me?" she snapped, losing the little bit of control she'd been holding onto. "Where did you guys even come from? This isn't a motorcycle bar, ya know. I have regular customers who wouldn't appreciate your obnoxious friends."

"Brothers."

"What?"

"They're my brothers--and you mean the old pervert and the divorced lady who were in here? Those are your regulars?" he asked, raising an eyebrow.

She flicked her cigarette to the ground.

"Fuck you. Go find somewhere else to drink." She pushed past his large frame and walked back into the bar. It seemed like things had actually quieted down in the short amount of time she'd been outside. Jen leaned against the bar and talked to one of the men.

Cam walked around to the back of the bar and tapped Jen on the shoulder. “Are you okay out here?” she asked.

“Yeah, I’m good...you know, you’re supposed to drop off the drinks--not wear them.”

Cam fumed her eyebrows together. “I'm aware.”

“I think I have an extra shirt in my purse from when I went out the other night.”

“I’m not going to be able to fit into your shirt. I’m fine. It’ll dry soon.”

Jen moved her mouth to the side as if thinking about saying something. “Amire might need some help with the kitchen.”

Thank god. If Jen could hold down the bar, Cam was fine with hiding in the back until these assholes left.

“Alright, let me know if it gets crazy again,” she said before heading to the kitchen.

Amire lifted a fry basket out of the hot oil and dumped a container of mozzarella sticks inside.

Cam grabbed an apron that hung on the wall. “Heard you need help.”

CHAPTER FOUR

Kit

He sat up in bed. It took him a minute to realize what woke him. *Bang, bang, bang.* The wooden, bedroom door shook as someone on the other side banged on it.

"That redheaded bitch wants to know where her car is," Jett yelled.

Kit ran a hand over his face. "Tell her it'll be done by the end of the day!"

He listened to Jett's retreating footsteps before resting back into the pile of pillows.

Blonde hair smacked him in the face as the girl beside him turned the other direction. He couldn't remember her name. She was a new club groupie. The clubhouse always had its fair share of women hanging around. Too bad for them, he wasn't looking to settle down with anyone...ever.

An image of the woman from the bar last night flashed in his mind. Green eyes, plump lips, and long, dark hair that he'd be more than happy to wrap his hand around while he fucked her from behind. His dick stirred at the thought.

"Time to go," he told the blonde, untangling himself from her naked body. His dick was hard as a rock, but there wasn't time to have another go around.

She groaned and opened one eye. "What time is it?"

He grabbed his phone that lay on the night-stand, sandwiched between empty beer bottles. "Past noon."

The bed creaked as he moved to sit on the edge. Bending down, he grabbed his sweatpants off the floor and pulled them on. There were a good amount of cars at the shop today. If he had been thinking last night, he would've left that bar earlier and gone to bed so he could get up early to start working on them. But instead, he'd stayed there, drinking with his brothers until the place closed. He was hoping he'd get another look at the owner. Cam. That's her name...at least he thinks that's what he heard the bartender call her.

The bed shifted again as the blonde sat up. Kit turned his head as the comforter fell away from her body. Her tits were huge with nipples so hard they could cut glass. He wished he hadn't been so drunk so he could remember what they'd felt like in his hands.

"Like what you see?" she asked.

If he jumped back into bed, she probably wouldn't hesitate to climb on top and ride him. Like most women hanging around the club, she was desperate. That was fine with him.

"Stick around the clubhouse. I might need some company tonight," he said, keeping it vague in case he changed his mind. He had a fight tonight, so depending on how it went, he might be too sore to fuck.

She stuck her lip out in a pout but got up from the bed before gathering her clothes off the floor. Instead of waiting for her to leave, he walked into the *en suite* bathroom and got in the shower.

The warm water washed away his morning grogginess. He should be hungover with how much he drank last night, but his tolerance was pretty high. He'd probably inherited his tolerance from his alcoholic father. He exited the shower and wrapped a towel around his waist before walking back into his bedroom.

The blonde was gone. In her place, in the center of the bed, was a piece of paper. Her phone number was scrawled on it in loopy handwriting. He shook his head and got dressed for the day.

The clubhouse was empty as he walked through it. His brothers were all probably at work. He squinted at the bright sun as he walked outside and made his way to the shop. Technically, Kit owned the shop, but everyone who knew anything about cars helped out. The shop wasn't attached to the clubhouse, but it might as well be since it was so close.

"Finally, that crazy bitch called twice today already," Jett said, his legs sticking out from under a Honda he was working on in the garage.

Kit sighed. "I'll have it done soon. We should

have gotten the new alternator in this morning. I can get it installed in a minute." He stood next to the car as Jett rolled out from underneath it. Jett helped out at the shop the most, which Kit was grateful for. Unfortunately, for his customers, Kit didn't work on anybody else's time. He got his work done when he got it done. Sometimes, he'd be working on cars until two o'clock in the morning and sometimes he didn't open until the afternoon. He had decided if he was going to own his own business, he was going to do it his way. Especially considering how many times he'd gotten his ass beat in order to raise the money to open the place.

"How was Jessica last night?" Jett asked as he stood up and dusted off his pants.

"Who?"

Jett chuckled. "Jessica. The one you took back to your room last night. Fuck, you didn't even know her name did you?"

Kit ignored him and walked into the lobby. Jett followed behind him.

"She's hot and isn't trashy like those other club sluts," Jett said.

Brown packages were stacked on the receptionist's desk. Kit pulled out his pocket knife and started to open them up, hoping to find the alternator he needed.

"Seemed just as desperate to me," Kit said to Jett.

"Nah, I think she's different."

"Then give it a go."

Jett leaned against the desk. "Are you going to the bar tonight?"

"Nah, I got a fight," he said. He found the box with the alternator and pulled it out.

"Oh shit, I forgot about that. I was going to put some money down."

"You still got time. Tony is usually taking bets until right before the fight."

The desk phone rang, and Jett walked off. "I'm not dealing with that redheaded bitch again."

Kit flipped him the bird before sitting down in the office chair and picked up the phone. "Ms. Granger, we have your ca..."

"Kit?"

It took him a moment to recognize his sister's voice because he hadn't heard it in so long.

"Megan?" he asked. His heart beat faster. It had been so long since he'd seen her last. She was always in the back of his mind. He never knew if she was even alive or dead.

"Yeah... I'm...um...close to Goldbeach."

"Where at?" he asked. If she were asking for a ride from a sketchy part of town, he'd hang up right now.

"At the airport... I was hoping you'd give your little sister a ride?"

"I'm on my way." He hung up the phone and grabbed his truck keys that hung on the hook next to the desk. "I'll be right back," he hollered at Jett, not waiting for his reply before walking out the door and getting into his truck.

He always kept it parked next to the garage because he rarely used it, but he wasn't sure what sort of state Megan was going to be in. He pulled out of the parking area of the clubhouse and onto the street. The airport was an hour drive from town, so he had plenty of time to calm his nerves.

Both he and Megan had grown up in Goldbeach but Megan took their upbringing much harder than he had. While he'd found the Savage Spades, Megan found drugs. It was an ongoing battle. Over the years, she'd stolen from him and taken advantage of every situation. She would say she was clean, but she never was. Four years ago, she moved out to California to be with whatever guy she was dating, and all contact between them stopped. So why was she here now? After all this time? He gripped the wheel tighter as he approached the highway. He could have asked her over the phone, but it was better to save his questions until he saw her in person. He turned up the radio to drown out his thoughts and continued his drive.

*****"Are you clean?" he asked an hour later as she stood next to the passenger side of his truck and tried to open the locked door. Her once, full cheeks were now hollowed out, but at least she looked alert. Her hair was brushed back in a neat ponytail and not greasy and stringy like when she was on one of her benders.

"Yes, I'm clean. Open the damn door, Kit."

She pulled the handle again and let out a breath.

"How long?" he asked through the open window.

"One hundred and eighty-five days and counting."

He pressed the unlock button, and she opened the door. She had a large bag over her shoulder that she threw inside before climbing into the truck. The minute she was inside, she pulled him in for a hug. He wanted to pull away from her and be stern, but he couldn't. Not when it'd been so long. She smelled like fresh soap and not like a crack house. Her body felt thin and fragile in his arms, and he was scared if he hugged too tight, he might break her. They hugged until the car behind him honked. She pulled away first and wiped a tear from her eyes.

"I've missed you so much."

"I've missed you too; let's get some food."

*****

They sat on a picnic table outside the BBQ joint. Megan wasn't scarfing down her food like she would if she'd been on a bender. Wherever she's been staying, they must be feeding her. Maybe she really was sober this time.

"What happened? Why are you back here?" he asked, finally cutting to the chase.

She set her pulled pork sandwich down and wiped her face.

"You can't just be happy to see your little sis?" she joked.

He narrowed his eyes at her.

"Fine, but it's a long story."

"I have time."

She let out a sigh and propped her elbows on the table. "When I left here, I moved in with Ricky--"

"That douchebag you were seeing?" he asked. He hadn't bothered to remember the guy's name at the time because it hadn't mattered. Kit had been happy to get Megan out of his hair at that point.

"Yeah, we lived together in California...and did a lot of drugs. We had our problems. I got arrested a few times. Ricky was an asshole most of the time."

"Did he put his hands on you?" Kit asked. His jaw clenched at just the thought. He hated to think his sister had put herself in that sort of situation.

"It's over, Kit. There's no reason to be mad now."

He scoffed. He had plenty of reasons to be mad. Years of anger still coursed through his veins. He'd be more than happy to take that anger out on someone who hurt his sister.

"Anyways, one night, me and Ricky had some friends over to the apartment. We were having a good time but I guess I took too much. I don't really remember anything after that besides waking up in a hospital bed. The nurses told me he'd dumped me right outside the doors. Fuck face didn't even come inside to make sure I didn't die." She shook her head and took a drink of her lemonade before continuing. "I was alone in a hospital bed, and the man I'd spent the last four years with didn't even care. No one was there. I was by myself. I knew once I was discharged, I couldn't go back to the apartment. What was I supposed to say to him? Anyways, the nurses talked to me about a treatment center. Apparently, I qualified for federal assistance so I could go for free. The first month was the hardest but after that, I started to feel like myself again. I was at the treatment center for three months, then I went to a halfway house. Now, I'm here. I want to find a job. Get on my feet. But the treatment center told me I need a support system...you're the only person I could think of."

He didn't say anything for a moment, letting it all sink in. He believed her. She finally hit rock bottom and had gotten help. Something he'd been trying to get her to do for years before she'd left.

"Whatever you need," he told her. It was hard to give her another chance after she'd screwed him over so many times in the past, but this time was different. She'd never gone to treatment before, much less admit that she'd fucked up.

Megan wiped another tear away from her face. "I love you, Kit. I'm sorry I've been a shit sister all these years."

He nodded. "I love you too."

They were both quiet for a moment, both lost in thought.

She pulled her food back to her and took a bite. "So, tell me what's been going on in your life all these years?"

"Nothing much. I opened a car shop by the clubhouse."

"I guess all that fighting money paid off. You're still a part of that club?" she asked, refusing to meet his eyes.

Megan always had an issue with the club, but he couldn't figure out why.

"Any lucky lady?" she asked, changing the subject before he could answer.

He laughed. "Many."

She scrunched up her face in disgust. "Too much information." She finished her food and pushed the plate away. "So really, when am I going to have a sister-in-law?"

"Never."

It was true. A woman wanted someone to take care of. Someone who could make their life better. He didn't have anything to offer a woman that would enhance her life, so there was no point in looking for someone to settle down with. The club sluts were more than happy to satisfy his needs. He was never going to be one of those guys with a two-story house and 2.5 kids.

He stood up from the table. "I'll get you settled at my apartment, and then I have to get back to work."

“Am I going to have to hear all about your many women?”

He laughed. “Nah, I’ve been staying at the clubhouse most nights anyways.”

She nodded and got up from the table, and they walked to the truck.

CHAPTER FIVE

Cam

She opened the door and stepped inside the bar. The massive bookbag weighed down her shoulders with all the textbooks she'd need to start school. Early this morning was the only free time she had to buy the stuff needed to start classes.

Since Jen had the day off, Cam had to open the bar. As she took another step inside, something crunched under her boot. Her body instantly froze up like the icicles that stuck to the gutters in the winter months. She lifted her boot and looked at the bottom. A shiny piece of glass was wedged between the grooves. Fuck. She dropped her foot before flipping on the lights. When the lights flickered to life, her chest tightened. Shards of glass covered the entire floor. The jukebox was facedown on the hardwood.

The tables lay on their sides as if someone had pushed them over. When Cam finally looked up from the mess around the floor, she saw him leaning against the bar. Her body flinched against her best efforts to show no fear. Ice filled her veins. He wore dress pants and a matching jacket over a black t-shirt, as if he was on his way to an upscale casino. He was tall but on the skinner side. He had dark hair that was pushed back out of his face. The most noticeable feature was his nose. So crooked, it had to have been broken several times.

Venom.

She took a step back, her boot crunching on more glass.

"I wouldn't do that if I were you," he warned, his voice filled with a threat.

She froze, waiting to see what he would say next. She knew this day was coming, but she still wasn't prepared for it. There wasn't enough money in the safe to pay him. She didn't have enough money if she sold everything she owned... except for the bar.

"It's been a while, Princess," he said. His voice sent a shiver down her spine like nails on a chalkboard.

"What do you want?"

"My money," he spat, his hands gripping the edge of the bar so tight his knuckles started to turn white. The sound of her heartbeat filled her ears.

"I don't have it right now," she said.

Although the bar had been doing better the last couple nights with the motorcycle gang here, she was still short. He smiled and started to walk towards her. She backed up until she hit the wood-paneled wall. He stood so close to her, his chest was almost touching hers. He reached out to touch a strand of her hair.

"Don't fucking touch me," she growled at him. This was bad...really bad. He could do whatever he wanted to her, and no one would be around to help.

He dropped his hand and stared at her. His dark eyes were glazed over. Being this close to him made her skin crawl.

"Feisty, aren't you?" he teased. His breath smelled like the inside of a trash can.

She breathed through her mouth.

"I'll get you your money. I just need time."

Time didn't bring more money in when it came to her bar. If anything, more time meant more money was lost. But she'd say whatever she needed to get Venom out of her bar.

"*Tsk, tsk.* You said that last time, and I haven't gotten paid. You see how that could be an issue? You could probably get some insurance money if this place burned to the ground." He looked around the room as if building an estimate in his head.

She shook her head. She had to keep the bar open. The bar was all she had right now. The last memories of her father were in this building. When she didn't say anything, Venom took a step away from her.

"My men will be by once a month to pick up my payment. Two thousand dollars a month, or I'll burn this place to the ground. Maybe with you in it. That's my last offer, Princess."

Fuck, that was a lot of money.

"Or...you can always take the option I gave you last time," he said, his eyes roaming over her body.

Her stomach turned, and she held down the urge to vomit all over the floor. The offer Venom gave her last time was to be his woman. He wanted her to live with him in his overpriced condo in Charlotte. She could still run her bar, and he'd pay for her to go to school, but he expected 'complete submission' from her. She didn't have a submissive bone in her body. She'd rather have Venom kill her than to be a sex slave to this disgusting man.

"I'll make my payments," she said, trying hard to keep her voice from wavering.

His face fell with disappointment, but he quickly masked it.

"You better," he said before leaving.

As soon as the door shut behind him, she let out a sigh of relief and swallowed the lump in her throat. She wouldn't let herself cry. She was stronger than that. Taking a deep breath, she grabbed her phone out of her pocket and called Jen. It was time to come clean.

*****

"Why didn't you tell us before?" Jen asked. She stared at Cam with pity in her eyes.

Cam hated it. She didn't want anyone to take pity on her, that's not why she was telling Jen and Amire the truth. It was for their safety. Venom could try to go after the people she cared about, which put Jen and Amire in the line of fire. She'd like to think that Venom would leave her crew alone, but she couldn't take any chances. Jen and Amire had nothing to do with the loan her father took out. They're innocent. *But wasn't she also innocent?* the voice inside her head questioned. She didn't have anything to do with her father taking out that loan. But she's the one who decided to keep the bar despite the risk, not her crew.

"I didn't want to worry you guys or put my stress on you. Venom is my problem. I'll figure out a way to deal with it. I just need you guys to do your job," she pleaded. She knew she was asking a lot of them.

"That's easier said than done. How am I not supposed to worry about you?"

Amire nodded in agreement. "Yeah, it's going to be hard to focus when I know that some guy is out to burn the bar down."

"I know, I know. Please just try. I'll figure it out."

Jen didn't look convinced, but after a moment, her expression softened. "Please, don't keep anything else from me, Cam. You know I'm here if you need anything."

That familiar lump in her throat reappeared. Jen opened her arms; Cam and Amire stepped in for a hug. Cam felt a weight lift off her chest. Dealing with everything alone took its toll after a while, and she was just happy that everything was out in the open. There may still be a dangerous threat circling over her head, but at least it was out in the open. She pulled back from the hug and wiped away the one tear that managed to escape.

"Alright, we should probably open the bar. Ernie is waiting outside," Jen said.

Jen grabbed the broom and started to sweep up the broken glass while Amire went back to the kitchen.

"You don't have to stay. You can go home and back to sleep," Cam said, feeling bad that Jen was at the bar on her off day.

Jen waved her off. "It's fine. I'm awake now anyway. Plus, I'm waiting for Hugo to leave my bed."

Cam grabbed one of the overturned tables and turned it upright. "Hugo?"

She must have slept well last night because she hadn't even heard Jen with someone.

Jen smiled. "Yeah, met him here last night."

Cam paused. "Don't tell me--"

"He's in the motorcycle club. They're called Savage Spades. He told me some more stuff, but I wasn't really listening."

At the mention of the guys from last night, Cam's mind instantly went to the tattooed-covered man that'd rammed his chair into her. She'd overreacted, but it hadn't just been the spilled whiskey that had pissed her off. It was the way he'd come outside and had the nerve to judge her for smoking. If he had just left her alone and allowed her to calm down, she wouldn't have snapped.

Cam sighed. "Come on, I'm trying to get rid of this motorcycle club, not give them more reason to come."

"They bring in money. Aren't you happy?" Jen asked with a raised eyebrow.

She should be, especially after Venom's reminder today. "They're loud and sending away all of our regulars. Plus, they forgot to pay their tab last night."

"Really?"

"Really. But I'm sure we'll see them again tonight. If they expect to drink anything, they're going to have to pay the tab from the night before."

CHAPTER SIX

Kit

The bar had been completely empty before they showed up. Now, the jukebox played some old country music that Gunner had selected, and the bartender was selling more beer than they probably had in years.

It was an older building with wood decor. There was a masculine feel to the bar, which was part of the reason it surprised him so much when he met the owner last night. He was keeping an eye out for her, but he hadn't seen her yet. It was stupid for him to even be waiting in anticipation for her to walk through the door. It was pretty clear from their first interaction that she wasn't the kind of girl to jump in his bed, so why was he still interested in her? It's not like he needed to chase after women. It was better for him to just focus his attention on the women at the club who jumped at the chance to spend a night with him. They were less complicated...they didn't expect anything from him that he wouldn't be able to give them. Other women wanted stability, time, money, etc. All things Kit didn't have.

"Iris' dance recital is next week," Zeke said

next to him. They were sitting in a corner booth facing the door.

"Oh, yeah, is she excited?"

Zeke shakes his head. "She's frustrated. Lily is coming over to help her practice tomorrow. That's completely out of my element, man."

Kit laughed. "What do you mean? You've never worn a tutu before?"

Zeke took a drink of his beer and flipped him the bird. Kit laughed again. Iris would be a handful for two parents, let alone one. She was a hyper and emotional kid. Lily was the one who suggested at Sunday breakfast one day that Zeke put her in dance class to get some of her energy out.

The sound of the bar door closing made Kit turn his head. Cam was dressed in a pair of cowboy boots and cut-off shorts. Her t-shirt was blue instead of white this time, and he wondered if she learned her lesson about wearing white to a bar. Her ass swayed as she crossed the room to go behind the bar. Long, black hair was piled on top of her head in a loose bun that bounced with each step. He bet he could make something else on her body bounce if she went home with him. He shook his head, trying to clear those thoughts from his brain. She wasn't one of those girls. She owned her own bar for crying out loud, so there was no way she was letting a biker take her home. It was ironic that he barely remembered the woman he'd taken to bed last night but every detail of Cam's appearance was etched into his brain.

"I'm going to grab another beer," Zeke said.

"I got it," Kit said before Zeke could get up. He got up from the booth and weaved through the tables.

Cam was already behind the bar getting ready for the night. He sat down in the barstool right in front of her. She rolled her eyes as soon as she got a look at him.

"What do you want?" she asked. Her voice had been laced with venom the night before, but now, she just sounded tired. He couldn't help the twitch of his mouth when she copped an attitude. Something about her was just so damn entertaining.

"Customer service isn't your strong suit, huh?"

She crossed her arms over her chest, and he couldn't help noticing how the gesture made her large breast look fuller.

"My customer service is fine when my customers actually pay."

"What's that supposed to mean?"

"Your gang--"

"Club." Calling the Savage Spades a gang was an insult.

She let out a sigh. "Your club didn't pay their tab last time."

Damn. Gunner must have forgotten last time they were here. Gunner kept a bank card on him that he used to pay for club activities. All of their monthly dues went to that bank account and they used it for times like these. Kit pulled out his wallet and passed over his credit card.

"Here. Put the tab from the other night on my card." He'd ask Gunner to reimburse him tomorrow.

Her green eyes looked down at the card and back at him. "All of it? Are you sure?"

"You want your money, don't you?"

She uncrossed her arms and grabbed the card before turning around to use the cash register. She came back with a receipt for him to sign. Goddamn, they'd drank a lot the other night. He signed the paper and handed it back to her. She tucked it under the register.

"Can I get a beer now?" he asked. She seemed to thaw a little now that he'd paid the tab.

"Bottle or poured?" she asked.

"Poured."

She grabbed a big mug from behind the counter and poured. She was sure to tilt the glass so there wasn't too much foam. He wondered how long she'd been working at the bar. She moved around like she had the place memorized. Like the same way he moved around his shop. She set the mug down in front of him, and he gave her a wink.

"See ya next time."

She twisted her face in disgust before turning around and helped her bartender slice some lemons. He carried the drink across the room and back to the booth where Zeke sat.

"You're not drinking?" Zeke asked him.

"I have a fight later tonight, remember?" he said.

"Hey, so what do guys think? This our new drinking spot?" Gunner asked from a couple tables away.

"Hell yeah," Zeke said.

The guys chimed in their agreement.

Kit looked over at the bar to see Cam with her mouth hanging open. He raised his beer with a smirk on his face.

CHAPTER SEVEN

Kit

"Congratulations, I heard you kicked ass last night," Jett said.

Kit winced as he lowered himself onto the barstool next to Jett. His whole body hurt. Like always, he still had plenty of bruises to show for his winnings.

"Yep, took home a grand."

Jett slapped him on the back, and his face twisted in pain. "Oops. Sorry, man."

The bar area of the clubhouse was full of people. Sunday was a big day for the club. Most of the town was closed today, and it was like an unofficial family day.

Zeke's daughter, Iris, ran up to Kit and handed him an ice pack. "Dad said to give you this."

Kit smiled and took the ice pack from her. "Thank you."

"Why do you need an ice pack?" she asked as she bounced from side to side. She wore a pair of jeans with a black t-shirt. Her hair was pulled into a loose, messy ponytail. It was apparent she was being raised by her father.

"I got in a fight," he told her. Several fights, to be exact. He'd stayed at the ring until his body started to scream at him.

Iris' eyes widened. "Whoa, did you win?"

He nodded. "Uncle Kit always wins."

She giggled before running away. Kit laughed and pressed the ice pack to his rib. His opponent got him good in the ribs. That was the only hit he let the guy get before Kit had landed a punch to the man's jaw. The feel of the ice pack was a relief to his inflamed muscles. His mind wandered to Megan. He needed to go by the apartment and check on her today. He believed she was sober, but anything could change in a matter of minutes, especially in a town where she knew who and where to get drugs.

Gunner's Old Lady, Lily, stood behind the bar looking for something.

"Where the fuck is that bowl?" she huffed.

Jett got up from the barstool, and Zeke took his place.

"What are you cooking?" Kit asked Lily.

She turned around and placed her hands on her hips. The Old Ladies cooked every Sunday. It was like the Savage Spades' version of church. There were only three Old Ladies at the moment. Gunner, Otis, and Ace were married. They were also the oldest brothers. Like himself, not many of the younger brothers were ready to settle down. Lily often complained about there not being enough women. The club groupies didn't count.

"Wouldn't you like to know," Lily said. Sunday dinner was always a surprise. "I heard Megan is in town."

He hadn't told many people about Megan being back. His eyes flickered to Zeke, who raised an eyebrow.

"She just got out of treatment," Kit told her.

Lily's face softened. "That's amazing. Is she staying with you?"

"For now. She says she wants to get a job and get on her feet."

"Well, don't rush her. Let her take her time. It's going to be an adjustment coming back here. Let her know I say hi, and she can stop by the house anytime she wants."

Kit nodded, but he knew Gunner wouldn't like that. Megan's past mistakes had burned a lot of people, and the last thing Gunner would want was for her to be around his wife. Lily could be too friendly for her own good.

"I'll let her know," Kit lied.

Lily smiled and walked out from behind the bar towards the kitchen.

"So, Megan's back?" Zeke asked.

"Yeah."

"You think she's sober this time?"

"I do, but I don't know how long it's going to last. She got into a good treatment center for free, and they told her she needed a support system. I'm not sure this was the best idea. Coming back to the town where her addiction started..."

He wanted his sister back, but more than that, he wanted her to be sober. He just hoped she was making the right decision coming back here.

"You can't control it, man. Megan's going to do what she wants, but give her a chance to prove to herself--and you--that she can be sober."

The front door slammed shut as Gunner walked into the bar. "Everyone in the meeting room," he said, walking past them to the room in the back.

Zeke and Kit shared a look before following behind everyone else to the room. Church was usually planned in advance and never on Sundays. Sundays were for the family. They took a seat at the big round conference table, waiting for everyone else to fill in. A couple of people were missing, but Gunner didn't seem to mind. Hugo closed the meeting room door once everyone was inside.

"I just got word that the new bar has some financial issues," Gunner said.

It took a minute for Kit to understand what Gunner was talking about--Cam's bar. Images of dark hair and plump lips filled his brain. He'd decided to spend the night alone last night because he was so sore, but his dick stirred to life as he thought about Cam. Wait, what had Gunner said? Financial issues.

Gunner looked over at Hugo, who cleared his throat. "Jen, the bartender, told me last night Cam owes a fuck-ton of money to Venom."

"What the fuck?"

"Venom, really?"

Venom was a snake that was slowly poisoning the town with drugs. He lived in the city, but his people didn't have a problem dealing their drugs in Goldbeach. The small town was probably a good portion of his business.

"Since when did Venom start loaning out money?" Otis asked.

Hugo lifted an eyebrow. "I don't know; apparently, the girl inherited the debt from her father."

What idiot would leave a debt like that to his daughter? He thought about Cam; she had no chance against a man like Venom. He would destroy her if she didn't find a way to get him the money.

"So, what are we going to do about it?" Ace asked.

"Do we have to do anything about it?" Kit asked.

Gunner glared at him.

"I'm just saying, why doesn't she sell the bar? Cut her losses. Is Venom someone we want to get involved with?"

He hated to be the one to say it, but when they burned down Old Timers, none of them expected to go to war with the town drug lord afterward. With Megan in town, he didn't want the club to be involved in any sort of conflict with Venom. Kit could smell trouble.

"We don't know how much she owes. Selling the bar might not be a solution," Hugo said.

"Like everything, we'll put it to a vote. Either we stay at the bar and claim it as our own or we turn our back." The way Gunner phased it; Kit already knew which way he was leaning. "All for making Cam's bar our own."

Everyone raised their hands except for Kit. Gunner stared at him until he reluctantly raised his hand.

"Then it's settled. We'll need a couple of people to watch the bar when we're not there. Kit and Zeke, you're on babysitting duty."

Kit clenched her jaw to keep his mouth shut. Gunner was doing this on purpose because Kit hadn't immediately agreed to the decision. He had enough on his plate with Megan back that he didn't need to worry about a problem that wasn't his. Plus, he had his own business to run.

"Kit, your shift starts immediately." Gunner hit the gavel on the table, dismissing the meeting.

Everyone filed out, and Kit went down to his room to grab his keys and wallet. When he turned around, Hugo was standing in the open doorway.

"Hey, I'm sorry about that. When I brought it up, I didn't know Gunner was going to make you sit at the bar all day."

"It's alright. I know you were just trying to help."

Hugo nodded. "Jen's a cool girl, and she was really concerned last night about her friend and the bar."

"Is she going to be your Old Lady?" Kit teased.

Hugo lifted an eyebrow. "Maybe, you never know."

Hugo walked down the hall to his room, and Kit went outside to get on his bike.

*****

When he pulled up to the bar, it was three o'clock. Closed signs hung on the doors of small businesses. He opened the wooden door of the bar. The smell of beer and cigarettes hit him in the face. The jukebox played quietly in the background. The glass screen was missing but it still worked.

Two people sat at the bar. One of them was an older man with completely white hair. The man looked like he was nearly falling asleep. On the other side of the bar was a lady in her forties. She had a cigarette in her hand and was watching the football game on the old TV behind the bar.

His dick twitched as his eyes landed on Cam. She leaned over the bar as she wrote something down on a notepad. Her position gave him a perfect view of her tits. Her hair was pulled up in a ponytail, but he preferred it down like the other night when he saw her. She looked up as he approached the bar. Her lips straightened into a flat line.

He smiled. Maybe this babysitting thing could be fun. He grabbed a stool and rested his elbows on the wooden bar.

"What are you doing here?" she asked, flipping the notebook over and grabbing a white towel from underneath the bar.

"Can't a guy just come in for a drink?" he asked.

She wiped down the already clean wooden surface. "Okay, what can I get for you?"

"You have Coke?" he asked.

She tilted her head. Her ponytail swished to one side, and for a second, he imagined what it would feel like to grab it. Fuck, he should have taken one of those girls down to his room last night so he wouldn't be fantasizing about someone he didn't even know. He was like a twelve-year-old boy seeing tits for the first time.

"Seriously, why are you here, and where is the rest of your gang?" she asked.

"The Savage Spades heard about your little problem."

Her face instantly drained off all colors. "I... don't--"

"Your friend spilled the beans, and lucky for you, Gunner decided your bar was worth protecting. Either Zeke or I will be here at all times." He winked at her.

To his surprise, she jutted her hip out and rested her hand on it. "I didn't ask for anyone's help or pity. I've been taking care of everything on my own, and this is not your gang's bar. It's mine. So thanks for the offer, but you can go back to your group and let them know I don't need anyone's help."

He took a moment to let his eyes roam over her body. He should have expected this amount of feistiness from her. It was the same attitude he got when he tried to apologize that first night when he'd stupidly knocked into her.

"Yeah, that's not going to happen. You're dealing with a mean motherfucker. Venom is not someone you wanna mess with."

"It's a little too late for that. Listen, we have an agreement. I'm slowly paying back the loan once a month, so there's nothing to be worried about."

"Can you afford the payments?" he asked.

She swallowed and lifted her chin. "Yes."

He scoffed. "Even if you weren't lying to me, you're a terrible liar. By the way, in our town, we don't let people like Venom come in and offer loans to business owners. So you won't be giving that piece of shit another dime of your money."

Her eyes widened. "Are you out of your mind? You just told me how dangerous he is, and then you tell me I'm not supposed to pay him the money I owe him."

"You don't owe him shit. Your dad did. That's not on you."

She snapped her mouth shut at his words. They stared at each other for a second, having a silent staring contest.

He got up from the stool. "I'll be over there

if you need me. Can I get extra ice in that Coke?"

He walked away to the booth in the corner of the room, feeling her eyes burning a hole in his back the entire time.

CHAPTER EIGHT

Cam

She tried her best to concentrate on the homework, but she could feel his eyes on her skin. Leaning against the bar, she stared at the sketch. It was a butterfly, but inside of the beautiful wings, she'd put different images that represented the butterfly's life. So far, she'd drawn the butterfly and a single piece of grass. She'd replicate the image on the computer when she got to school in the morning. It would be helpful if she had her own computer. The one in the back office was too old even to install Photoshop. She'd tried.

"That one is good to go. You can call him to pick it up."

Her head snapped up at the sound of Kit's gruff voice. He spoke into the phone, giving orders to someone. It was probably something illegal that she shouldn't listen to. He looked even better than he did the other night despite the bruises that covered his face. Another sign that the motorcycle club was trouble. Were they really trying to help her or was she just getting into another bad situation? Being in the middle of a war between a motorcycle club and a drug dealer wasn't her idea of fixing the problem. Why would they volunteer to help her when they didn't even know her? His tattooed arm flexed as he lowered the phone away from his ear. Her body started to heat up as she stared at his broad shoulders. What was wrong with her? She hadn't bothered to look at a guy in months, and now, she was practically drooling on the counter.

"Beer," Ernie grunted, breaking her from the trance she was in.

Kit turned his head towards her and gave her a knowing smile.

Fuck, she was caught. She turned away from his piercing eyes and cocky grin before she poured a mug of beer for Ernie. The front door creaked open as she set the beer down. The man looked to be in his early thirties. He was leaner than Kit but with just as much muscle definition. Slicked back, jet black hair covered his head. She let out a sigh of relief; this must be Zeke. The guy Kit said would be watching over the bar too. Zeke had to be better company than Kit.

Zeke smiled at her before walking over to the booth Kit was in. They slapped hands before swapping places. Kit came up to the bar and set his empty glass down.

"See you around, sweetheart."

She glared at his back as he walked out. She was going to kill Jen.

*****

"Jen!" Cam yelled before slamming the front

door of the house shut. Why did Jen think it was okay to tell people about her loan to Venom? It wasn't some small-town gossip. This was her life.

Jen bolted out of her bedroom and into the living room. Cam stood with her arms crossed over her chest.

"What's going on?" Jen asked, her eyes wide in panic. She was dressed in pajama bottoms and a loose t-shirt, which meant she was staying home tonight. Cam was too annoyed with her to be surprised that Jen was actually staying in on a summer night.

"What's going on? You told your one-night stand about Venom. Now, I have a man-bun wearing bodyguard stationed at my bar."

Jen shook her head. "Wait, slow down. What happened?"

Cam sighed and went into the kitchen to sit at the table. Jen followed and sat in the chair across from her. The bar closed early on Sundays, so it was only midnight. She took a deep breath before starting to explain. "One of those motorcycle guys came into the bar. The one with the bun--"

"Kit," Jen chimed in.

"Huh?"

"His name is Kit. Hugo filled me in."

The same way Jen filled Hugo in on all her personal business. Cam fought the urge to roll her eyes.

"Right, so Kit came in and told me that you

told Hugo about Venom."

Jen put a hand to her mouth. "Oh shit, I'm so sorry, Cam. I was tipsy last night. Hugo and I were just deep in conversation. It must have just slipped out."

When wasn't Jen tipsy? She loved her best friend, but she couldn't help being annoyed. Jen got to live carefree, always doing what she pleased. On the other hand, Cam constantly felt the weight of the world on her shoulders, getting heavier and heavier with each passing day.

"Well, now we'll have one of their club members at my bar twenty-four seven. According to Kit, I'm not supposed to pay Venom any money."

"Um, this is a good thing, right?" Jen asked.

"No, it's not a good thing!" she hissed. "Venom is not someone I want to mess with. They are just making everything more complicated."

Why couldn't Jen see that? Not paying money you owe to a very dangerous man was not a good idea. He'd come after her. The only question was when, and would the motorcycle gang be there to protect her when all hell broke loose?

"Listen, you don't have the money to pay Venom anyways, and now, you have an entire motorcycle club looking out for you."

"I didn't ask for that."

Jen waved her off. "Just relax. Maybe Venom won't want to bother with the bar once he sees that he'd have to go to war with the Savage

Spades."

"Savage Spades?"

"That's the name of the motorcycle club."

"How long did you and Hugo talk for?" Cam asked, her anger starting to melt away a little bit.

Jen smiled. "A long time. I'm going over to his place tomorrow night. I think he lives at this big clubhouse that they all hang out at."

Cam scrunched up her nose. "What, like a frat house?"

"I guess I'll find out when I go. He said there's a bar inside."

Cam threw up her hands. "Then why don't they drink at their bar?"

Jen shrugged.

Cam shook her head. "I need to get to bed."

"You have class in the morning?"

"Yep, don't forget you're opening."

She said goodnight to Jen and headed to the bathroom to take a shower. Despite the hot, stuffiness of the house, the hot water felt great as it ran across her tight muscles. She never noticed when she was bunching her shoulders up until she finally had a chance to relax them. After getting out of the shower, she walked to her bedroom in a towel. She pulled on a pair of pajama bottoms and a t-shirt.

As she lay in bed, her mind wandered to her future. What did she want out of all this? All the stress and tiredness couldn't last forever. How long was she going to hang on to the bar? What about when she graduated school? Her father would have wanted her to sell it as soon as he died. But she couldn't think about that in the midst of the funeral and her grief. The bar never brought in much money, but at least she had enough to live off of.

For a moment, she let herself dream of what it would feel like to not have to worry about anything. To have a life like Jen's, where she could go to work and come home without having to think about inventory or bills. Taking a deep breath, she closed her eyes and went to sleep with that fantasy dancing in her head.

*****

"Do you need help?" Cam yelled to Jen over the loud rock music. She'd come in early, planning on getting some paperwork done before taking over for Jen. But with the way it was crowded with their new regulars, she might have to push paperwork to the side. Again.

Jen shook her head. "I got it. Do what you have to do."

If this was going to become a regular thing, she might have to hire another bartender...and cook. Cam bit down on her lip, deciding if she really should sit in the office, or if she needed to help out.

"Go, I got it," Jen said, shooing her away.

"Thanks. I'll be done as soon as I can." She walked to the back office and sat down to start working on the liquor order for the week.

The deposit also had to be prepared to take to the bank tomorrow morning. An hour later, she counted out the last of the cash and stuffed it into the deposit envelope. It was the most money she'd deposited in months. The teller at the bank would probably think she stole it. The money would just be taken out soon to pay the bills and make payroll. At least she could enjoy the sight of money in her bank account for a little bit. She stuffed the deposit envelope back in the safe. As she closed the safe door, a loud crash echoed through the building. Jumping up from her chair, she dashed out of the office.

On the floor of her bar, two men rolled around, throwing punches. The sound of skin hitting skin made her stomach turn. The rest of the motorcycle club stood around in a semicircle, watching the fight unfold. Her nostrils flared, and her muscles tensed up. This was funny to them?

"Are you fucking serious, right now?" she snapped, but no one seemed to be paying her any attention.

The bigger man now had the smaller one in a headlock. She took a step towards the fight, ready to break it up. Strong arms wrapped around her waist, preventing her from taking another set. She looked over her shoulder to see that Kit was holding her back. Her nose filled with his woodsy scent, and she hated to admit that being this close against his body gave her a sense of calmness.

"You're going to get yourself hurt," he said.

"Get them the fuck out of my bar. I'm not having it." Her face was hot and probably bright red.

He nodded. "Okay."

He let go of her and waved his hand at Jen's new boy toy, Hugo. On cue, Hugo stood up and pulled the men apart.

"Alright, that's enough," Hugo said, stepping through the circle and standing next to the two men. That didn't stop the bigger man from laying another punch on the smaller one. Hugo grabbed the bigger man and hauled him off of the smaller one.

"If you're going to fight, take it outside!" she added, putting her hands on her hips.

An older man in the back of the group stepped forward. "You heard the lady, take it outside."

Both guys stood up on their feet. Hugo gave them a push so they would walk outside. After a moment of silence, everyone went back to their drinks. She turned to Kit, who was still standing behind her with a smug grin on his face.

"You think that's funny?"

"You could thank me."

She turned on her heels and walked back to the office, his footsteps following behind her. Her fingers itched for a cigarette.

"Thank you? Why would I thank you?" she asked, continuing her walk into the office and sitting down in the black office chair. She looked up at Kit. He had his arms crossed over his chest and was leaning against the wall. If she wasn't so annoyed with him, she might acknowledge the fact that he looked good tonight. Under his leather cut, his black t-shirt squeezed his biceps.

"Because if I hadn't waved Hugo over, they probably wouldn't have stopped until someone tapped out."

Is that what happened at their bar? At this clubhouse that Jen had told her about? She wouldn't be surprised.

"Is that how you got that?" she asked, tilting her head towards the bruise just below his eye.

"Something like that."

She smiled. "I bet you got your ass kicked."

He chuckled. "Not a chance."

They stared at each other for a moment. Fuck, he was good looking. It had been so long since she'd gotten close to a guy. The smell of Kit's cologne alone could turn her on. Too bad he was an arrogant jerk, or she might go out with him. What was she thinking? She had enough to focus on without the added stress of a relationship.

He opened his mouth to say something, but she beat him to the punch. "You should go unless you want to see me go through paperwork for the next hour."

He nodded and walked back to the floor, leaving her alone.

CHAPTER NINE

Cam

It was nearly closing time when she finally came up for air. Jen had offered to stay for the rest of the night and manage the bar. Cam'd tried to argue with her, but Jen had insisted.

"I'm going to the clubhouse tonight anyways. I might as well make some money while I wait around for them to finish drinking here," she'd told Cam.

It'd given Cam the chance to catch up on all the outstanding stuff she'd meant to get done.

"Hey," Jen greeted her.

Cam smiled at her and grabbed a cup before pouring herself a Coke. "It looks like everyone's leaving?"

"Yeah...well, going back to the clubhouse."

Amire came around the corner in the midst of untying his apron.

"Hey, Amire, you've been quiet tonight," Cam said.

He followed her action and grabbed a cup to fill with soda. "The new customers keep me busy. Those guys can eat. Oh, by the way, we're running low on a few things."

"Shit. Make a list, and I'll try to see if we can get an early delivery."

She also made a mental note to see if she could afford to hire another person. She didn't want Amire and Jen to feel like she was working them to death. Plus, if one of them were out sick, there's no way she'd be able to handle the bar and kitchen alone with as many guys that were here tonight.

"So...I was thinking..." Jen started.

"Oh no," Amire said before taking a sip of his soda.

Jen stuck her tongue out at him. "I would really like some company tonight..."

"Oh, fuck no. Hugo is your company," Cam said. There was no way she wanted to spend her night sitting around at a bar across town with the same people who were just here. If she wanted to do that, she would have kept her bar open longer.

"Come on, Cam. You're going to let me go somewhere alone with a bunch of big motorcycle guys?"

"You want to go!"

Jen puffed out her bottom lip.

"Ha!" Amire said. "Guess that means you're going. You two have fun. I'm going to finish in the kitchen."

Amire walked away as Jen continued to stare at her with those big, puppy dog eyes.

"Jen, come on. I want to go home and get some sleep," she said. Her body was so achy, all she wanted to do was get in a hot shower then curl up under the covers.

"Just come out for a little bit. We don't have to stay long."

"You're not spending the night?" Cam asked, raising an eyebrow at her.

Jen shook her head. "No, I have plans for breakfast with my mom in the morning."

Jen's parents lived about an hour outside of town, so she was able to see them often. Jen raised an eyebrow at her waiting for an answer. God, she was tired, but she knew Jen would return the favor if she had asked.

"Fine, but just for a little while."

Jen squealed and pulled her in for a tight hug. "You are the best! I owe you."

"Yes, you do. Now, let's clean up so we can get this over with."

Jen cleaned behind the bar while Cam took care of the lobby. Amire finished before both of them and left. Once they finished, Cam locked the door and followed Jen out to her car.

"We can get your truck after I get back from breakfast with my mom," Jen said as they climbed into her small, silver car.

"That's fine." She wanted to sleep in tomorrow anyways. Her class didn't start until eleven o'clock, so that meant if they got out of the bar early enough, she might get seven hours of sleep.

She leaned her head back against the headrest as Jen followed the GPS. If she allowed her eyes to flutter closed, she'd be asleep in a matter of minutes. As they traversed onto a dirt road in the middle of nowhere, her eyes flickered to Jen. "Are you sure this is the right address? There's nothing out here."

"This is what Hugo gave me."

As Jen got closer, Cam realized why she never saw the clubhouse before even though it was huge. The long, sheet metal building stretched across a couple of acres of land. The building wasn't one color. It looked like pieces of the building had been added on over the years. It was in a valley, so Jen had to turn off the main road and drive down a steep hill to get there. As soon as they pulled up, Cam could hear the music from inside. The same kind of rock music they played out of her jukebox. The front door to what must have been the bar part was wide open, allowing the music to spill out. The entire area was surrounded by tall stadium lights, which probably kept the coyotes and other wild animals away. It would have been impossible to find the place without the stadium lights on. Everything around the clubhouse was pure wilderness.

"Damn, this place is huge," Jen said as she turned off the car.

"Like a cult," Cam grumbled.

Jen laughed. "I heard that. It's not a cult; it's a club."

"Tomayto. Tomahto."

They got out of the car, and she followed behind Jen into the clubhouse. Cam's short cowboy boots thudded against the wooden porch. As they walked inside, she noticed the whole place was wood. It looked like an actual cabin. She imagined it would be a beautiful place to sit by the fire in the winter. The bar was double the size of Cam's, and she wondered again why they would come all the way out to her bar to drink.

"Let's get a drink," Jen said, looping her arm through Cam's and steered her to the bar. She was surprised to see that not only were there other women in the bar, but also, they were all half-naked. Most of them wore short halter tops and denim skirts with flip-flops. Their makeup was heavily applied. A blonde haired woman gave them a dirty look as she and Jen sat down at a stool.

"What can I get for you, ladies?" the guy behind the bar asked. He looked like he was barely eighteen. Not old enough to be bartending.

"Can I get a gin and tonic?" Jen asked.

"Coming up, and for you?" the boy asked.

"Just a Coke," she said.

"Got it. One gin and tonic and one rum and Coke."

"Oh no, I--"

He walked to the other end of the bar before she could correct him. Whatever, she probably needed a drink anyway to get through the next hour or so since she was going to be stuck at this place.

"It's crazy how big this place is," Jen said.

"Yeah, it's so far out too." The location of the clubhouse made her suspicious. As if maybe the motorcycle gang wanted to keep themselves hidden. As she looked around the bar area, she started to wonder what they did. Were they really just a group of guys who liked to ride motorcycles together? The way Kit called them his brothers the first night she met him made her think it was more than that.

"Hugo said they all have bedrooms here, and there is a car repair shop on the corner that Kit owns."

Two drinks were placed in front of them. Cam took a sip, feeling the burn as it went down her throat. There was way more rum than Coke in the drink, and she made a mental note not to order a second one.

"Oh, there's Hugo. I'll be right back," Jen said before hopping off from the stool and taking her drink with her.

Cam sighed and took another sip of her drink.

"You don't look too happy to be here," the young bartender said. He placed both hands on the bar top and leaned against them. He was a cute kid with chubby cheeks and messy brown hair.

"Between you and me, my friend dragged me here."

"Ah."

"How old are you?" she asked him. Her curiosity was getting the best of her.

He smiled, showing off a dimple on the left side of his face. "Depends, are you a cop?"

"Nope, but if I were, I probably wouldn't tell you." She took another sip of her drink.

He laughed. "Fair enough. I'm seventeen."

She coughed, nearly choking on her drink. "What the hell are you doing bartending?"

"I'm prospecting."

She raised an eyebrow. "Um, what?"

"You're new to this whole motorcycle thing, aren't you?" he asked.

"I wouldn't call it that. I'm just here with a friend."

He nodded. "Well, a prospect is someone who wants to be patched. Like, be a member of the Savage Spades. Basically, you have to do a lot of shitty jobs and put up with a bunch of bullshit until Gunner and everyone else thinks you're ready to be an official member."

"Wow, you guys take this thing seriously."

"Well, yeah, it's a lot of work to be a part of the Savage Spades. The club is much bigger than just here in North Carolina. There are chapters everywhere."

She tilted her head to the side. "And why do you want to be a part of the motorcycle gang again?"

He grabbed a towel and started to wipe down the bar. "It's not a gang; it's a club. A lot of members don't have a real family. The Savage

Spades is the only family they know. We take care of each other. Even if I'm stuck doing the dirty work, I know it'll pay off when I get patched."

She took a sip of her drink as she processed the information. It still didn't make sense to her. Why would a seventeen-year-old kid want to do a bunch of shit for a group of grown men just so they would accept him into a club?

"Aren't you in high school?" she asked.

He shook his head. "Dropped out last semester. That's when I found the Savage Spades. According to Gunner, I need to re-enroll by the end of this month if I want to think about getting patched."

At least they were making him go back to school. Does that cancel out the fact that they also had him bartending at seventeen?

"I'm Oscar, by the way." He stuck out his hand for her to shake.

"Cam," she said, placing her hand in his.

A man at the end of the bar said something to the kid. She couldn't make out his words.

"I'll see you around, Cam," he said before dropping the towel and heading towards the end of the bar.

Cam sipped her rum and Coke and turned on the stool to look out on the small dance floor. Jen swayed back and forth with Hugo even though it was a fast-paced song. Although Cam was annoyed that Jen had dragged her here, at least she was happy.

After spending the next hour playing on her phone and talking on and off with Oscar as he worked, she got up to find Jen. The bar was starting to quiet down. She'd watched a few of the guys leave with a barely-clothed woman on their arm. She found Jen in a corner booth snuggled up next to Hugo.

"Cam!" Jen exclaimed.

Oh shit.

"I was looking everywhere for you!" Jen shouted.

Cam turned to Hugo. "How much did she drink?"

Hugo was the biggest of all the guys she'd seen at the clubhouse so far. He also had a tattoos on his neck, which made him intimating, but his face was that of a big teddy bear.

"A lot," he admitted.

"Fuck, she was supposed to drive me home."

"I heard Kit say he was about to head out. I'm sure he'd give you a ride," Hugo suggested.

"Oh no--"

"Hey, Kit," Hugo yelled across the room.

Heat traveled up her neck to her cheeks as embarrassment took hold. She hadn't seen Kit since leaving her bar. She turned around to see him coming out of a room.

"What's up?" he asked Hugo as he approached the table. His eyes flickered to hers briefly. He was probably wondering what the hell she was doing there.

"You leaving? Jen can't drive, and Cam rode with her," Hugo explained.

Kit looked at her, a smug grin on his face.

"She told me we'd be here for an hour or so. She was supposed to drive me home," Cam said.

"Mmm, so you couldn't get enough of us."

"You know what, forget this," she said. She turned on her heels and walked to the exit. She'd find some other way to get home. Fresh air hit her face as she walked out onto the porch.

"Come on, I was just messing with you," Kit said from behind her.

She turned around and crossed her arms over her chest. She didn't know why she was so embarrassed by being stranded in Savage Spade territory, but she was.

"Come on. My truck is parked on the other side of the clubhouse. Unless you wanna get on the back of my Harley?"

The thought of pressing her tits into Kit's back as they drove through these dirt roads had her clenching her thighs together. He walked past her, giving her no choice but to follow behind him. They rounded the big building to a darker part of the clubhouse.

"So really, why did you agree to come out here?" he asked her.

"Jen begged me to go with her because she wanted to see Hugo. She didn't want to come alone."

"Ah, I'm a little disappointed. I thought you

missed me so much you couldn't stay away."

She snorted. "In your dreams."

But as she looked over at him, she couldn't help being impressed. He wasn't wearing his leather cut like usual. Instead, he was in a pair of gray sweatpants and a black t-shirt. He was the only guy besides Jason Momoa that could pull off a man-bun like that. When they got to his truck, she opened the passenger door and realized the truck sat a lot higher than Big Blue. It took her two tries to get inside all while Kit sat in the driver's seat and laughed.

She flipped him the bird once she was finally in the seat.

"I was going to help you, but you got it."

"Yeah right."

"Give me your phone," he said.

"Excuse me?"

"I'm putting my number in it. In case something like this happens again."

"It won't." There was no way she was coming out here with Jen again. Jen owed her for this one.

"Would you just give me your phone?"

Reluctantly, she handed over her shitty, out-of-date iPhone. He typed in his information and then handed it back.

"I can give you a ride if you ever need one. I own the car shop, so I work when I want."

She nodded and tucked the phone back into her pocket. "Thanks. So why do you guys come to my bar to drink if you have a bar right here?"

"Most of us are at the compound too often. It's nice to get out and take a short ride sometimes." He shot her a half-smile. "Besides, maybe we just like to bother the towns people every once in awhile."

He started the engine and drove back towards town.

CHAPTER TEN

Kit

"Where are you going this late at night anyway?" she asked him from the passenger seat.

"Work."

She raised an eyebrow and scrunched up her nose. "Work where?"

He didn't answer. He had a couple of fights tonight that he needed to get to. He usually gave himself more of a break between matches, but Tony had called him and said that a lot of people were taking an interest in him. There was a lot of money on the table. If he could get enough, he could help Megan get back on her feet. Maybe send some to his piece-of-shit dad so that he could buy candy or whatever shit they buy in prison.

"Okay..."

"I can't tell you," he said. It wasn't only the fact that the fighting ring was illegal, but also, he didn't trust Cam yet. Especially not with that kind of information. She had a stick up her ass, and he got the feeling she'd turn her nose up at the thought of someone using their fists for money. Which didn't make sense considering her hands were just as dirty since she was involved with a drug lord.

"Okay, whatever, it was just a question."

They drove the rest of the way in silence until they got to her bar, where her blue truck sat out front.

"Thanks for the ride," she said.

He waited until she got in the truck and drove away before turning around and going to the fighting ring.

Gravel crunched under his tires as he pulled up to the driveway. Tony's family owed acres of land where the fights took place. Kit had been going to the same spot for years. The cops knew about it, but they chose to turn their heads. Whenever the ambulance was called because someone took too hard of a hit, there was never any follow up. If he had to guess, Tony gave the cops a nice cut of each fight so he could keep the thing going.

Kit got out of the truck and walked onto the grassy area. People stood around, holding beers and watching the fight. Inside a spray-painted, red circle were two shirtless men throwing punches. A set of bleachers and some lawn chairs surrounded the property. He spotted Tony sitting on the bleachers, a red baseball hat on his head.

"You got some fights for me?" he asked, taking a seat beside Tony. Tony bounced his leg, and his hands were tucked into his pants pocket as if he was cold, even though it was eighty degrees outside.

"Yeah, yeah. You're up against Carl and Jax," Tony said.

"Fuck." He'd take down Carl with no problem, but Jax was a big motherfucker. Kit reached into his pocket and handed a roll of dollar bills to Tony. He always betted on himself, no matter what.

Gasps sounded from the crowd, and he turned to see that one of the guys had fallen to the ground. Tony stood up and waved his hands.

"Jeremy wins!"

The man named Jeremy flexed his muscles and let out a roar even as blood dripped from a cut on his forehead.

Tony slapped Kit on the back. "You're next."

*****

"Kit?" Megan's voice echoed through the garage and into the waiting area where he was flipping through paperwork that didn't make any sense to him.

"In here," he shouted.

Megan rounded the corner with a massive smile on her face, but it slipped as she caught sight of him.

"Oh my god, what happened?" she asked, coming around the desk to get a closer look at his face. He'd won the first fight, but he hadn't been as lucky with the second one. He should have let his body recover more before agreeing to two fights in one night. By the second fight, his muscles were exhausted, and he hadn't moved fast enough to dodge the guy's fists.

"I'm fine."

"Fine?" She put her hands on her hips. "Who the fuck did you get in a fight with?"

He didn't answer. Understanding dawned on her.

"Are you fighting still?" she whispered.

"Just when I need some extra money," he said, not feeling like getting into it with her.

"And what the hell do you need extra money for? You don't even stay at the apartment you rent."

"That seems to be working out in your favor now," he said.

Her face twisted with hurt.

"Megan, that's not what--"

"You know what? You won't have to worry about me for long. I got a job today. So have fun getting a concussion. God forbid someone tries to care about you."

She walked away, and he rubbed a hand over his face. He'd apologize when she calmed down. The last thing he wanted was for her to feel like she was an inconvenience. She came back to Goldbeach for a support system, and he needed to be that for her. That might be harder than he thought.

The phone on the desk rang. "Kit," he answered.

"Hey, are you on your way?" Zeke asked.

He raked his brain, trying to figure out what

he was talking about.

"To Cam's bar. I have to go to Iris' dance recital, remember?" Zeke said.

"Oh shit, I completely forgot. I'm on my way." He hung up and grabbed the keys to his motorcycle. As he drove down the dirt road, he realized he needed to get his head straight. Maybe he had been hit too hard last night if he forgot that he had to be at Cam's. This babysitting thing was a pain in the ass. He needed to be at the shop, working on some of the cars. Between Megan, his fights, and Cam, he was falling behind. Customers were starting to notice.

He parked his bike out front and walked into the empty bar. The same two people as always sat in the stools. Zeke was at a table in the middle of the room. Kit slapped hands with him.

"My bad, brother, I completely forgot."

Zeke waved him off. "It's cool. The recital hasn't started yet, but I wanted to get there early. She was nervous about it yesterday."

"Anyone else going?" Kit asked.

"Gunner and Lily."

Kit nodded and watched as Zeke left. When he turned around, he was disappointed to see Jen behind the bar instead of Cam. Cam, at least, made this babysitting thing a little bit enjoyable. When he wasn't talking to her, he could at least stare at her ass. He had to admit it had been a long time since he was so fascinated with one girl. He hadn't even slept with anyone else since meeting Cam.

Usually, no one was able to hold his attention, but he found himself wanting to talk to her. She was the opposite of all the girls who hung around the clubhouse. She wanted nothing to do with the Savage Spades. It was refreshing. He walked to the bar and took a seat on the stool.

"Oh, hey, Kit," Jen greeted. She was definitely more friendly than Cam.

"Hey, where's the boss lady?" he asked.

"She's at home working on some homework. I think she'll be in later."

"She's in school?" he asked. It seemed like she lived at the bar; it was crazy to think she was taking classes too.

"Yeah, she goes part-time up at the college. You want something to drink? Maybe help with all that bruising on your face?"

He smiled. "No, I'm okay, thank you."

She nodded and went back to cleaning up. Kit scrolled through his phone for the next hour as he waited. He sent a quick text to Megan:*I'm sorry about earlier. I'm happy you're back in town.*

The door opened, and Cam walked in, dressed in a tight shirt that dipped low enough that if she bent over the bar, he'd probably get a good look at her rack. Her face was red as if she'd been running around. She didn't even notice him sitting there.

"Hey, sorry, I would have been here sooner, but I had to swing by the school to talk to one of my professors."

"It's cool; it's not like we're busy."

Cam looked around and caught his eyes briefly before turning back to her friend.

"Let me put my stuff down, and you can go."

He watched her ass as she walked to the back. A man with dreadlocks came out of the kitchen and grabbed a drink.

"You think I'll get sent home?" the man asked Jen.

"Yeah, probably. We've been slow all day," Jen replied.

There was no way Cam could have paid off Venom if her business was slow like this. The front door opened, and a tall man walked inside. His eyes were bloodshot-red. Kit sat up straight and watched the man.

"What can I get you?" Jen asked as the man plopped down in a stool.

"A shot of vodka," he slurred.

Jen hesitated, as if deciding whether or not to serve him before grabbing a shot glass and pouring.

Cam came back from around the corner with a smile on her face. "Okay, you can go. I got it from here."

After setting the shot glass in front of the man, Kit watched as Jen grabbed her purse from behind the counter and said goodbye to Cam. The cook went back in the kitchen, and Cam walked over to him.

"Your turn to babysit? I like the other guy

better," she teased, leaning over the bar enough that he could see down her shirt.

He grinned. "You like him better, but you don't even know his name?"

"His name is Zeke," she said proudly.

"You're learning."

He liked this teasing side to her.

"You get beat up again?" she asked.

"Something like that."

She reached her arm out, and her fingers lightly grazed his face. Her hand was soft and gentle. Despite how much his bruises hurt, her touch was light. He stared into her soft, green eyes. She realized her mistake and quickly pulled her hand away.

"I'm sorry."

"It's okay, a lot of women have problems keeping their hands off me."

She rolled her eyes and pushed off the bar.

"Another one," the tall man at the end of the bar demanded. He slumped over, resting his head on the bar.

"I think you've had enough," Cam said, walking over to the man and putting her hands on her hips.

"Stupid bitch," he mumbled.

Kit stood to his feet, waiting for what the man would do next.

Cam shook her head. "Get the fuck out of my bar." She reached to grab his empty shot glass, but he grabbed her arm as she tried to pull it away.

Kit's jaw clenched. He took two steps and was immediately in front of the man.

"Let her go," he said.

The man dropped her arm and stood up from the stool. The man was taller than Kit but nowhere near his size. He smelled like a brewery and had probably gotten cut off at another bar before coming here.

"You think...you're tough guy?" the man slurred. He pulled his fist back, but Kit acted first.

He pushed against the man's chest, causing his unbalanced body to slam against the bar. Kit grabbed him by the collar of the shirt. The man twisted back and forth, trying to get loose as Kit dragged him toward the exit. He opened the door and pushed the man outside so he fell on the warm sidewalk.

"You come back here, it's going to be a lot worse."

Kit slammed the door on the man, and when he turned around, Cam was looking at him with wide eyes.

The older man at the end of the bar placed two fingers in his mouth and whistled. "That's what I'm talking about!"

"Thanks for that," Cam said as he got closer.

"That's why I'm here."

She smiled. "You want some food?"

"Yeah, what you got?"

CHAPTER ELEVEN

Cam

"What are you drawing?" Kit asked her before plopping a fry in his mouth. She caught the flash of his tongue ring as he ate.

"Something for school."

He reached across the bar and slid the notebook towards him before she was able to stop him.

"A butterfly?" he asked.

Her cheeks heated up.

"It's for school," she repeated, trying to grab it from his hands, but he kept it out of her reach.

"You draw?" He raised an eyebrow at her, and she wished she knew what he was thinking.

"Sometimes, but this is for a project. I just have to map it out before I replicate it on the computer."

He studied the drawing for a moment. Each minute that passed made her palms more sweaty.

"Can you just--"

"Draw me a tattoo," he said.

"What?" she asked, obviously mishearing him.

He set the notebook down on the bar and slid it back to Cam. "I've wanted some new ink anyway." He rolled up his sleeve and showed her an unmarked piece of skin.

"I can't--"

"Why not? You just have to give the drawing to the tattoo artist, and he'll ink it on me."

"You want me to draw something that's going to be on your body forever?"

It was a crazy idea and a lot of pressure. But her mind started to fill with ideas. What would represent Kit? Maybe a dangerous animal or a clown. Her lips twitched as she thought about a big, ugly clown tattooed on his arm.

"Why not?"

"That's a lot of pressure."

"If I'm not worried about it, you shouldn't be either. Just draw something for me, and I'll stick it on." He slapped the naked skin where the tattoo would be. He said it so naturally, as if getting a tattoo wasn't a big life long decision.

"Fine…when I have time."

He smiled at her but left her alone for the rest of the night.

She hated to admit that Kit made the last few hours of the night entertaining. She had to send Amire home early since it was so slow, but he didn't seem to mind. Kit waited outside as she locked up. He leaned against the brick wall as she shut the door. With his hands in his pockets, he walked with her across the street to her truck.

"Thanks again for taking care of that guy," she said. She could have taken care of it herself, but it felt good to have someone else do the dirty work. He took a step closer to her. Woodsy cologne filled her nose--a mix between pinecone and mint. A feeling of comfort washed over her.

"I told you. We protect what's ours."

Her eyes went to his lips, wondering how they would feel against hers. Fuck, she had to stop thinking like that. It had been so long since she'd even thought about a guy that she was practically foaming at the mouth. But even if that wasn't the case, Kit was the most beautiful man she'd ever seen, even with his leather cut and man-bun. Two things she thought she'd never be attracted too.

She cleared her throat. "So when do you think the club will be back?"

"You miss us?" he asked, that cocky smirk across his face.

"No, I just want to make sure I'm here to help out if Jen and Amire get too busy."

"I'll ask the guys and let you know."

She nodded, and they stood there for a moment staring at each other. His baby-blue eyes were such a contrast to his darker appearance that she couldn't help feeling lost in them.

"Goodnight, Cam," he said.

"Goodnight."

She turned away from him to get in her

truck. He took a step back to allow her space to get in. She awkwardly waved before turning the key in the ignite. Instead of rumbling to life, the only sound was a small *click*. She tried again but only got the *click*.

Kit knocked on her window. "Pop your hood."

She did as he asked before climbing out of the truck to join him. He lifted the hood and inspected the engine.

"What is it?" she asked.

He started poking around and moving parts. "I'm not sure. It could be your alternator, but I'd have to test it to see."

She laced her fingers together. "How much is that going to cost?"

He pulled the hood down and wiped his hands on his jeans. "It just depends. Don't worry about it right now. Let me take you home."

She looked over at the motorcycle parked in front of her bar.

"On that thing?" she asked.

He chuckled. "Unless you prefer to walk."

Her feet were aching from standing on them all night. Walking back to the house was not an option. Her stomach twisted with a mix of excitement and nervousness as she followed behind Kit to his motorcycle. He handed her a helmet and showed her how to secure it on her head. The brush of his fingers against her skin as he buckled the chin strapped caused goosebumps to rise over her arms. He climbed on and instructed her to get on behind him.

"Hold tight," he said.

She awkwardly wrapped her arms around his waist, feeling his body heat against hers. He chuckled, but she didn't get a chance to ask what he was laughing about before he took off.

She squeezed him tight, no longer embarrassed by their closeness. The wind hit her in the face as he drove through the streets. He leaned the bike so far over when they turned she was scared she might fall off.

"You okay back there?" he yelled.

She nodded her head against his back. Her face rubbed against the leather of his cut. She watched as they got closer to her neighborhood, and she loosened her grip as he slowed in front of her house.

"How did you know where I live?" she asked as she climbed off the bike.

"How was your first ride?" he asked, ignoring her question.

"Scary...but good."

She couldn't deny that she kind of liked the wind running through her hair, but more than that, she loved being that close to Kit. He helped her remove her helmet.

"Oh shit."

"What?" he asked.

"I have class in the morning, and I have no way to get there."

She looked in their driveway to see that Jen's car was gone. She was probably at the clubhouse with Hugo.

"Call me in the morning. I'll drive you."

She bit her lip, wanting to say no, but she didn't have any choice. She was already on academic probation and couldn't afford to skip any classes.

"Thank you."

"No problem. Are you sleeping here alone?" he asked, looking past her at the dark house.

"I think Jen is probably with Hugo. I'll be fine. Thank you for everything tonight."

He looked skeptical but nodded. "See you tomorrow, Cam."

*****

The next morning, Jen pulled into the driveway as Cam waited on the lawn for Kit. She wore a big, gray hoodie that reached to her knees.

"What are you doing out here?" Jen asked, closing her car door. She looked at the empty spot in front of the house where Cam usually parked the truck. "Where's Big Blue?"

"He broke down last night. Kit is coming to pick me up."

Jen's lips pulled up into a smile.

"It's just a ride to school," Cam said.

"Uh-huh, I could have driven you."

"I knew you were at Hugo's. I didn't want to bother you. Kit offered."

"I'm sure he did."

"Seriously, it's just a ride. I don't have time for anything serious. I have way too much shit going on as it is." Cam had to admit she was warming up to Kit. He wasn't the arrogant guy she thought he was when they first met. But that didn't change the fact that she wasn't ready for a relationship right now. A relationship would only further complicate her life.

"So you're saying if you didn't have all this shit going on, he'd have a chance?" Jen teased.

Cam ignored her. Jen laughed to herself as she went inside.

A minute later, Kit pulled up. She was relieved he didn't bring the motorcycle. It only took her one try this time to get into the truck. It wasn't until she was fully seated that she looked over at him. He wasn't wearing his leather cut today, and she wondered if he only wore it when he was riding the motorcycle. He wore a pair of gray sweatpants, and she couldn't help but notice the impressive outline under the material.

"So..." he said as she pulled her eyes away from his lap and up to his face. "I think I can get your truck fixed."

He pulled away from the curb and onto the street.

"Really? For how much?" If she waited a week to pay her liquor distributor, she could spend a couple of hundred dollars to get Big Blue fixed. Any more than that and she was going to be shit out of luck.

"Free. I'll fix it on one condition."

"I'm not sleeping with you--"

"Whoa, why would you think I'd ask that?" His eyes flickered between the windshield and her.

She shrugged. "I don't know. You're a guy..."

He shook his head. "Anyways, I'll take your truck to the shop and get it fixed up, but you have to agree to go camping with us this weekend."

She instantly scrunched her nose up. She hadn't gone camping since she was a kid. The only memory she had of camping was not being able to shower and using one of those weird, outside toilets.

"Why do you want me to go camping?"

"The Savage Spades do it every year, and it's a big deal. According to Hugo, Jen is going too, so no one is going to be in town."

It did make her nervous to think about not being able to reach anyone when she hadn't paid Venom this month. That would be the perfect opportunity for him to pull something crazy. On the other hand, she didn't feel comfortable being out in the woods with the motorcycle club yet. The only guys she knew were Zeke, Kit, Oscar and Hugo.

"And you'll fix my truck?" she asked.

"I'll have it back to you by Monday," he said. They pulled up to the school, and he parked in the first spot. Turning to her, he waited for an answer. She didn't have a choice at this point. Her only other option was to stay at home where she'd be vulnerable to Venom and shell out the money to get her car fixed by someone else. She would have to close the bar. Ernie could drink somewhere else for one night.

"Okay, I'll go. Do you guys have a cabin or something?"

He shook his head. "No, we do real camping, none of that pussy shit."

She laughed.

"We're leaving tomorrow night at seven. Most of the guys have work during the day so we're leaving later than usual."

"I'll be ready."

*****

Her overnight bag sat on the bed as she looked through her drawers for clothes to wear on the camping trip.

"You might want to grab a bathing suit. There might be a lake," Jen said, leaning against Cam's open bedroom door.

"Did Hugo tell you that?" Cam asked, looking up from her drawer.

Jen shook her head. "No, he's been pretty secretive about the whole thing, but I brought my bikini just in case."

Cam opened her top drawer, grabbed her turquoise-colored monokini, and threw it in the bag.

"I'm so happy you're going. I thought I was going to be all alone with those guys."

"I wouldn't be going unless Kit offered to fix Big Blue for free."

"You like him." The floor creaked as she crossed the room and sat on the edge of Cam's bed.

Cam shrugged. "He's cute, but...I don't know."

"Stop overthinking everything. I know you think you're not allowed to have fun for some crazy reason, but I'm telling you, it's okay to enjoy your life."

Cam leaned against the dresser and locked eyes with Jen. "I know. I want to have fun; it's just hard with the bar and trying to get through school."

"How about this weekend, you just forget about all that? Bring Crazy Cam. Leave bar owner/ student Cam at home."

Cam smiled at her. "Fine."

Jen was right. She deserved a break from running the bar and doing homework. Even if it was only for one night, she should embrace it.

Jen threw her hands in the air. "That's what I'm talking about. Oh, hey, by the way, what tent are you in?"

Cam paused. "I don't know... I didn't think about that."

Jen stood up from the bed. "You probably have your own anyways."

She hoped so, considering Kit hadn't mentioned anything about her tent. Did he expect them to share one?

*****

Once she was packed and ready to go, she rode with Jen over to the clubhouse so they could leave from there. When they pulled up, there were more cars than she had seen before. Usually, it was just a bunch of bikes, but there were a couple of sedans and a few other trucks, including Kit's.

"How many people are going?" she asked Jen as they climbed out of her car.

"Everyone associated with Savage Spades, I think."

They walked inside to the bar area. Three women dressed in shorts and t-shirts sat in one of the booths. The men stood around the space all laughing and talking like it was one big family. The room smelled like bacon, as if lingering from this morning. She hadn't noticed a kitchen before, but maybe there was one in the back.

Hugo spotted them from across the room and walked over. He wrapped an arm around Jen and kissed her lips. Cam had to admit they did look cute together. She just hoped they'd last. With Jen's dating history, Hugo could be out on the curb any day now.

"Hey, Cam," Hugo greeted, once he pulled away from Jen.

"Hi, Hugo."

"This is everyone that's going?" Jen asked him.

He looked around the room. "I think so. None of the club sluts are invited. It's a family thing."

"Club sluts?" Cam asked Hugo.

"Yeah, the girls that hang around here in barely any clothing... Open to any guy that gives them even a small amount of attention."

She wondered if Kit had sex with the club sluts. It made sense that he would. But her stomach still turned at the thought of his hands on someone else. She had no reason to feel jealous. It's not like he promised anything to her or even asked her out on a date or anything. Is that what she wanted? The only reason she was here right now anyways was to get her truck fixed. The air around her shifted. She knew it was him from the woodsy scent that filled her nose.

"You ready?" he asked, his husky voice coming from behind her.

She turned around to face him. His baby-blue eyes stared into her. A warm sensation wrapped around her body, and instead of fighting it off or denying her attraction to Kit, she allowed the feeling to spread. She'd told Jen she was leaving her bar owner/student Cam at home, and she meant it. She did deserve to have some fun.

"Yeah, I was going to ride with Jen--"

He shook his head. "No, part of the deal is riding with me."

She crossed her arms over her chest. "You didn't say that."

"I'm saying it now."

She smirked at him. "Fine."

"It's a two-hour drive. Can you hold on that long?"

"We're taking the bike for two hours?" she asked, her eyes widening.

He laughed. "I'm just kidding. I'm taking the truck."

She slapped him on the chest, making him laugh harder.

"Are you that scared of the bike?"

"No, but I'm scared to ride on it for two hours."

"You'll get used to it."

She opened her mouth to ask what he meant, but a man at the front of the room cleared his throat. Everyone quieted and turned their attention to the bald man with a gray beard at the front of the room.

"We're leaving in the next ten minutes. If you're riding, check-in with Jett. Otis, you have all the tents?"

"All loaded up," a skinny man with glasses replied.

"Coolers?" the bald man asked.

"Got 'em," Kit said, loud enough so everyone could hear.

"Alright, I'll see you all on the road."

CHAPTER TWELVE

Kit

"I'm surprised, I'd take you more for a rock 'n roll man," Cam said from the passenger seat. She wore a pair of dark jeans with holes in them. He had trouble keeping his eyes on the road and not on her creamy skin peeking out.

"I listen to a little bit of everything."

She pulled down his sun visor to find a line of CDs. "And you still have CDs?"

"I never got rid of my collection. I listen to them every so often."

She flipped through the disks, reading off titles as she went. She seemed to be in a better mood today than he'd ever seen her in. Maybe she was starting to feel comfortable around him, which was what he desperately wanted. She had a wall that was built higher than the sky, and she might finally be lowering it. His focus should be on Megan and his shop, but lately, his thoughts kept going back to Cam. She took up all the space in his brain.

He cleared his throat. “So your dad--”

“What about him?” she asked, not looking up from the CDs.

“He owned the bar before you?”

She nodded her head. “He and my mom were separated. The only time my mom would let me visit him was during the summers. My mom and I don’t have the best relationship. As soon as I turned eighteen, I moved down here with Dad. We had a good two years or so together before he got sick. I was going to school full-time and helping at the bar when I could, but after he got sick, everything changed. I took over all the major stuff for the bar...started skipping classes. It was a hard time.”

Her voice held steady as she talked to him, as if she’d rehearsed the story in her head. She put the CDs back.

“I’m sorry,” he said.

“Thank you. It was tough since we finally had the close relationship I wanted so bad as a kid, and as soon as we did, he died. I just wish I had the time to grieve. There was so much to do with the bar, and then I found out about Venom’s debt...”

He wasn’t sure what to say. Life was tough like that sometimes, and it was never fair.

“What about your parents?” she asked him.

“My mom died when I was little. I don’t remember her much. My dad did the best he could, but his drinking got real bad. He’s in prison for drunk driving. He killed two teenagers on one of those back roads. He was drunk out of his mind."

She looked down at her hands. "I'm sorry."

"It is what it is. I have my sister and the Savage Spades, so I always have a family."

"You have a sister?" she asked.

He nodded.

"Will I meet her?"

"She's not a big fan of the Savage Spades for reasons I will never understand. She's staying at my apartment until she can get back on her feet. She's a recovering addict."

He held his breath, waiting for her to respond. His life wasn't sunshine and rainbows. It was a fucked-up journey. The only people who knew his story were his brothers.

"So when did you join all this?" she asked, waving her hand around.

"When my dad first started drinking." He laughed. "Gunner made me work my ass off to get my patch."

He thought about all the bullshit he had to put up with. One day, Gunner had him ride all over North Carolina just to get Lily a burger she'd been craving. At the time, she'd been four months pregnant. They'd lost the baby a couple of weeks after that.

"Is the bartender...um..."

"Oscar?"

"Yeah, Oscar. Is he coming on this trip?"

Kit smiled. "Yeah, we'll make him do all the dirty work."

She shook her head and scooted down in the seat.

'Tired?" he asked.

"Very."

"Sleep, I'll wake you when we get there."

*****

The sun cast a pink glow over the wooded area as the line of trucks and bikes pulled into open spots around the property. Kit parked facing the main area; that way, when Cam woke up, she could see the bonfire ahead and follow it. He had no intention of waking her up. Even with only spending a short amount of time around her, he knew her schedule was packed. She probably had very little time to sleep. The other day, he'd picked her up at nine a.m. after just dropping her off at one that same morning. He admired her work ethic, but he also saw all the things she didn't discuss. How she cracked her neck throughout the day as if her bones were hurting. After she closed down the bar, she always took one shot of whiskey, like a reward to herself for getting through another day. He wished he was the kind of guy who could save her from the stress cycle, but he didn't have money or anything to offer her.

Zeke knocked on his window. Kit looked over at Cam to make sure the sound didn't wake her. She didn't even flinch. He got out of the truck and softly closed the door.

"She asleep?" Zeke asked. He carried the black carrying case for his tent in one hand and a pink, unicorn backpack in the other.

"Yeah, let her sleep." Kit rounded the truck and grabbed his tent. He was surprised Cam hadn't asked about their sleeping arrangement. There was only one tent, and he hadn't planned on bringing another one.

He looked over at Zeke. "Where are you setting up?"

"I'm not sure yet. Probably close to the fire. Iris likes to be around all the older girls." Zeke smiled as he talked about his daughter.

Kit could only imagine the stress that Zeke was under raising that girl by himself. He was probably terrified, but he had a whole family that looked after Iris. If Zeke was working at the shop for extra cash, Lily was more than happy to grab Iris from school.

"Let's set up yours first, and I can figure out where we're going to set up," Kit said before following Zeke to an open area near the bonfire pit. Oscar was already busy chopping the wood.

"So things getting serious with you and Cam?" Zeke asked, setting down his bag and unzipping it.

"Not really. I told her I'd fix her truck for free if she came." Kit grabbed one of the poles and started putting it together.

"Ouch."

He played it cool, acting like it didn't bother him. He couldn't offer Cam anything to fix the mess she was in, but at least he could give her one night away from it all, even if he had to hold her truck hostage to do it. After setting up Zeke's tent, Kit decided to set up their tent closer to the lake. By the time they finished, it was nearly dark outside. In an hour or so, it would be so dark he wouldn't be able to see the hand in front of his face. He and Zeke were walking back to the bonfire when Jen approached them.

"Where's Cam?" she asked, crossing her arms over her chest, as if ready for an argument.

"In the truck, sleeping."

"You left her in the truck?!"

"She was asleep. Let her sleep," Kit said.

"She's going to be mad when she wakes up and finds out she's been sleeping in the truck while everyone else set up."

Hugo came up behind Jen and wrapped an arm around her waist. It surprised Kit at how affectionate he was. Hugo wasn't one to hook up with any of the club sluts, but Kit also hadn't seen him take an interest in any other girl.

"Are you guys all set up?" Kit asked Hugo, ignoring Jen.

"Yep, we're on the other side of the fire. Wanna get some beers?" he asked.

They all walked over to the center of the property, where plastic chairs were set up around the fire. Kit reached in the large cooler and pulled out a beer before getting comfortable in a chair. Hugo sat next to him with Jen happily perched on Hugo's lap.

A crunchy sound made Kit turn his head. Cam rubbed her eyes as she walked across the field. She had thrown on his jacket. It hung over her body like a blanket. She'd also pulled her hair up in a ponytail. None of the club sluts, or short-term relationships he'd had, held a candle to Cam. She was beautiful without trying. She sat down in the plastic chair next to him, her eyes still glazed over from sleep.

"Hey, there," he greeted.

"Hey, why didn't you wake me?" she asked.

"I figured you needed the sleep."

She looked around the field, as if taking in her surroundings. "Yeah, I did."

"Is it time for Crazy Cam to come out?" Jen asked over his shoulder.

Cam laughed. "I guess so."

Jen threw her a beer, and Cam caught it. Kit looked back and forth between the two of them.

"Crazy Cam?" he asked Cam as she carefully opened the beer so it wouldn't bubble over.

Jen answered him instead. "She left bar owner/student Cam at home. This is Crazy Cam; you haven't met her yet."

He raised an eyebrow at Cam. "Is that so?"

She smiled. "Yep. I've pledged to have fun and enjoy this weekend."

"Well, we're going to need more alcohol," he said. He stood up and wheeled the entire cooler over to the bonfire.

"Should we be worried?" Gunner yelled at

Kit from the other side of the fire.

"Yes; yes, you should," Hugo answered back.

Two hours later and he understood what Jen meant when she said he hadn't met Crazy Cam yet. She was happy and carefree, and he didn't think it had so much to do with the alcohol but more to do with permitting herself to have fun.

"Let's swim," Cam said over the loud country music that Hugo was playing through his battery-powered speaker.

Some people had already gone to their tents for the night. Others stood around talking with beers in their hands. He looked towards the lake. It was too dark to see anything, but he doubted anyone was down there. No one wanted to swim in pitch black...besides Cam.

"Why don't we wait until the morning?" he suggested.

She stood up from the chair and started to jog towards the lake. "Are you scared?" she called out to him over her shoulder.

With a sigh, he pushed out of the chair and started to run after her. She squealed when he wrapped his arms around her waist.

"Let's wait until the morning when we can see," he whispered into her ear. The feel of her warm body against his made his dick twitch. He tried to keep it under control since he had her pulled in front of him, and she would feel it if he got rock hard.

"No, I'm hot. Water feels good." She wiggled

out of his arms before skipping to the small area of sand that led to the water. He could barely make out her frame in the darkness.

"I don't have my trunks," he yelled after her.

"And I don't have my suit."

It took him a minute to realize what she was suggesting. Looking behind him, they were far enough away from the bonfire that no one could see them. He heard a splash, and his decision was made for him. He walked the rest of the way until he was standing at the entrance of the lake. In the moonlight, he could make out Cam's head bobbing in the water.

"Come on, it feels good...unless you're scared," she teased.

He looked down to see the clothes she was wearing laying on the sand. His dick hardened instantly, and he stripped out of his clothes, leaving them in the sand next to hers. The water was cold, but it was a nice contrast to the hot heat of the summer. Rock and sand indented the bottom of his feet as he moved toward her. When he got close to her, she smiled at him. He could see her clearly now. Her face was usually a mask of annoyance or stress, but now, she just looked relaxed and happy.

"You got me out here. Is this where you drown me?" he asked.

She laughed. "I could. I hadn't thought about it."

He took a step closer to her, wanting to feel her soft skin. She didn't step back as he expected her too.

"I like you, Kit," she admitted.

That was a relief considering he usually had no idea how she felt about him. He was glad he wasn't the only one who felt their connection. He reached under the water and grabbed her waist. Fuck, her skin felt so soft. She pressed her breast against his naked chest, and his dick was at full attention. He moved his hands down to grip her ass, and she let out a moan.

"That feels good," she whispered. God, he wanted her so bad right now. She reached between their bodies and started trailing her hand down his chest.

"Wait," he said, stopping her in her tracks. It would be so easy to give her what she wanted, but he couldn't. As much as he wanted to lift her up and impale her with his hard cock, it wasn't right.

She puffed out her bottom lip. "Why not?"

"You're drunk."

A laugh bubble up from her throat. "I'm fine." She started to move her hand again, but he latched onto her wrist.

"If you still want to have sex in the morning, we can. But when I do fuck you," he said, and leaned down to whisper in her ear. "I'll make sure you remember it in the morning."

Goosebumps rose across her skin. She pressed her big tits harder against his chest; her hard nipples rubbed against him. He'd fantasized about this exact moment so many times he just wished she was sober so he could act on it. Hopefully, she felt the same way in the morning.

"Please, Kit," she whispered.

He swallowed. "I can't. Not when you're drunk."

She pushed away from him to give herself some distance before splashing him with water. "You're no fun."

He laughed. "Come on, let's go back to the tent."

When they got out of the water, she didn't want to put her clothes back on, so he carried her to their tent buck naked. He was relieved that everyone had gone off to bed, and the fire was slowly dying. Even if someone was awake, they couldn't see her. He laid her down in one of the sleeping bags, and she passed out. He got in his sleeping bag and went to sleep, dreaming about the beautiful woman next to him and hoping that she'd feel the same way in the morning as she had tonight.

CHAPTER THIRTEEN

Cam

The sound of voices woke her from her dreams. She blinked a few times, taking in her surroundings. It took a minute for her to remember where she was. She sat up, but her head started to pound, so she laid back down. Her mouth was so dry you'd think she'd been living in a desert.

"Hey there." The voice made her jump, which only made her headache worse. Kit lay in the sleeping bag next to her. He was shirtless…or just naked.

She couldn't tell because the sleeping bag covered the lower half of his body. She looked down at her own body, realizing she was naked in the sleeping bag.

"Uh…did, we?"

He shook his head. "No, despite you begging for it." He wiggled his eyebrows at her.

"Oh my god, tell me I didn't."

He laughed. "You did, and you pouted when I told you no."

She ran a hand over her face as her cheeks heated up with embarrassment. She only had bit and pieces of memories from last night, but she definitely didn't remember trying to get Kit to have sex with her.

"We went swimming?" she asked, feeling her damp hair.

"Kind of…more like skinny dipping."

She couldn't believe she did that. "How much did I drink?!"

He laughed. "Enough to get wasted." He got out of his sleeping bag, and she was relieved to see he had on a pair of sweatpants. He grabbed her bag from the corner and handed it to her before putting on a t-shirt. "I think everyone already ate breakfast, but I'll try to find us some food."

He unzipped the tent and left, giving her some privacy. What she needed was a warm shower and a hairdryer. She slipped on the swimsuit she'd packed and threw a sundress over it. She attempted to brush through her tangled hair before giving up and throwing it in a bun. Once she looked decent enough, she left the tent.

There were a couple of big picnic tables set up where people were sitting. A handful of kids ran around the large campsite playing tag. She didn't remember seeing any kids last night, so they must have already been asleep. The fire was out, but people still sat around in the plastic chairs talking. She spotted Jen sitting at one of the picnic tables with a plastic coffee cup in her hand. Cam crossed the campsite and sat down next to her.

"Oh, hey sleepyhead," Jen said, and laughed.

"I need a soda."

Jen chuckled. "I think Kit just left to get you guys some food. Gunner's wife made breakfast this morning, but these men eat so much, it was gone fast. So, spill what happened last night."

Cam groaned. "I'd tell you if I remembered. I have no idea. Kit said we went skinny dipping--"

"Oh my god! I knew you were into him!"

"*Shh*," Cam said, looking around to make sure no one could hear Jen's outburst. "I didn't say I like him... I was drunk."

"Yeah, okay. Don't try to use that excuse on me. Drunk Cam is Honest Cam, and you have a thing for Kit--admit it."

"Fine, maybe I think he's hot...like really hot." She thought about his naked chest this morning and the tattoos that went all the way down his left arm. No wonder she tried to have sex with him in her drunken state. But it wasn't just about his looks. His sense of humor drove her crazy at first, but now she liked that cocky grin that spread across his face before he told a joke. What he told her about his dad and his sister on the drive over was heartbreaking, but he still gave his sister a place to live. He was paying for an apartment he didn't even live in. He had a big heart behind all that joking and arrogance.

"See, I knew it. You try so hard to make excuses for why you can't have a relationship but you know what I think it is? I think you're scared."

"Scared of what?"

"Scared of actually trusting someone to help you. You're scared that the moment you start to lean on someone for support, they'll vanish."

Jen's words were like a knife to her chest. Was that true? Was she terrified to let Kit be a partner in her life? She thought about her strained relationship with her mom. Her mom was never someone she could rely on. Then, when she'd moved to Goldbeach, she'd had an actual parent for a little while. Her dad had been an amazing man. When he was alive, she had a place to stay, and she could help out at the bar when she wanted extra cash. All she had to worry about was finishing her degree. Everything changed once he got sick. In a matter of months, she was back to struggling to take care of herself.

An older woman sat down at the end of the picnic table. "I am ready to get out of here and get in the shower," the woman said.

"Ditto," Jen replied.

The woman smiled at them. It was a comforting smile that reminded her of a grandmother. There was something warm about her presence that put Cam at ease.

"Are you Kit's Old Lady?" the woman asked.

"Yes, she is," Jen replied with a fat grin on her face.

Cam shot Jen a glare. "I'm Cam. I run the bar."

"Nice to meet you, Cam, I'm Lily, Gunner's wife. Sorry for assuming. I just got excited when I heard Kit was bringing someone this year."

"Does he usually not bring anyone?" she asked, already knowing the answer.

Lily shook her head and let out a sigh. "Most of the guys don't. I don't know what's wrong with these men. We need more women in the club."

"How many women are there?" Jen asked.

"Just a few of us."

Cam looked around. All the women seemed to be at least five years older than her. The female to male ratio was definitely out of whack.

"Those hoochies don't count," Lily said.

Jen choked on her coffee, clearly holding back a laugh.

"Hey, Lily! Where are the plates?" a small boy called out.

"Looks like I'm needed. Hopefully, I'll see you girls around. We always have brunch on Sundays at the club, so don't be afraid to stop by." She patted Cam's leg before leaving the table.

After Kit came back with a bag of McDonald's and a Coke for her, they ate and packed up the tent. Jen and Hugo stayed to spend another night.

Kit pulled his truck up in front of her house and helped her grab her bag from the back.

"I'll start working on your truck," he said.

"Thanks."

They stood there for a moment before she

cleared her throat. "So about us..."

He smiled that cocky grin of his. "What about us?"

"Are we like...dating?"

He laughed. "I had to hold your truck hostage just to get you to go on this camping trip."

She smiled. "True. How about you come over sometime...to the house? Not now, but maybe one day when I'm showered and not smelling like lake water--"

She shut her mouth before she could babble on any longer.

He raised an eyebrow. "You sure?"

All she'd done up to this point was give him a hard time, so she wasn't surprised by his response.

She nodded. "Yeah."

"I'll see you tomorrow."

She turned and walked toward her house. "Goodbye, Kit."

*****

The sound of the floorboards creaking woke her out of her sleep. Her heart raced as she tried to calm her breathing. Jen wasn't supposed to be back until the morning. Venom. She'd been so wrapped up in her life she almost forgot about the threat dangling over her head. She looked around the dark bedroom searching for anything she could grab as a weapon. Venom would probably have a gun if he wanted to kill her, but the sick bastard probably intended to kidnap her and use her as his personal sex slave. Her hands were sweaty as she grabbed a hold of the lamp on the bedside table. If she was going down, she'd go down fighting. She quietly crept out of bed but paused as she heard laughter.

"*Shh*, Cam is sleeping."

Cam sighed with relief at the sound of Jen's voice.

She opened her bedroom door to find Jen and Hugo pushed up against the wall in the hallway. Jen turned her head at the sound of the door opening.

"Fuck, I'm sorry, Cam. I didn't mean to wake you." Jen's eyes moved to the lamp that Cam had clutched in her hand. "You were going to attack me with a lamp?"

"No, I was going to attack the intruder with a lamp." Cam flipped on the hallway light and blinked a few times for her eyes to adjust. "I thought you weren't coming home until the morning."

"We were, but most of the guys ended up leaving, and it's scary out in the woods alone. Plus, I wanted to shower."

"Maybe call next time?" Cam suggested.

Jen nodded. "I'm sorry. I didn't mean to scare you."

Cam walked past them into the kitchen to grab a cup of water. Her eyes flashed to the clock on the wall. It was only 10 o'clock. She barely remembered falling asleep. After drinking her water, she left the kitchen. Jen and Hugo had retreated to Jen's room, so Cam went back into her own.

*****

She sat at the kitchen table with papers surrounding her. After class, she came right back to the house to get caught up. Jen was closing the bar tonight, so she had plenty of time to work on the homework that was piling up. Her phone vibrated next to her. Kit's name flashed across the screen. She pressed 'decline', to ignore the call. Jen had offered to drive her to and from class today, so she hadn't seen Kit. She was only able to focus on her homework for another minute before her phone started to buzz again with his phone call. She set her pen down and answered.

"Yes?"

"You didn't need a ride this morning?" he asked.

She usually called him if she needed a ride or texted him the night before. It was still strange that she was regularly asking him for rides, but she didn't have much of a choice. Kit said she'd get her truck back by Monday but he was obviously dragging his feet. She didn't want to ask about it since he was fixing it for free.

"No, Jen drove me."

He was quiet for a moment. It sounded like a garage door opening in the background.

"Are you at work?" she asked.

"About to be. Wanna come hang out with

me?"

She looked at the table in front of her. "I have a lot of homework."

"Bring it. I'll pick you up."

She let out a sigh. "What are we doing?"

Their relationship was turning into more than him just watching over the bar, but she couldn't blame him for that considering she was the one that apparently tried to convince him to go skinny dipping.

"Let's not make this complicated. Either you come here, or I'll come over there."

"Don't you have to work?"

"I own the place. I can work when I want."

She laughed. "I bet your customers love you."

"I'm on my way," he said before hanging up on her.

She looked down at the holy t-shirt and pajama bottoms she had changed into after class. She shouldn't care, but for some reason, she didn't want Kit to see her as a complete slob. Fuck. She got up from the couch and went into her bedroom. Laundry had piled up so she was limited on clean clothes. Choosing her typical shorts and t-shirt, she was able to change, apply a bit of makeup, and pull her hair up in a ponytail before the doorbell rang. She took a deep breath before opening the front door. Kit stood on the other side, just as tall and muscular as always. She doubted that he did anything to get ready to come over besides roll out of bed and get dressed. It wasn't fair.

"Are you going to invite me in, or do I have to stay out here?" he asked.

She opened the door wider and waved him inside.

"It's small, but it works for us," she said to Kit as she led him through the house. It was strange having him in her personal space. He looked out of place next to their feminine decor.

"Why is it so fucking hot?" he asked as they got to her bedroom.

She sat on the edge of the bed. "Landlord hasn't fixed the air conditioning."

He removed his cut. "How long has it been like this?"

"Almost the entire summer."

"You should have told me."

She shrugged. "I thought you just fixed cars."

He smiled that cocky grin of his that had her clenching her thighs together. "I can fix anything."

She raised an eyebrow. "Oh yeah?"

He took a step toward the bed, and she had the urge to scoot back, but she forced herself to stay still. He leaned down and planted a kiss on her lips. His lips were soft like pillows, and they felt like heaven on top of hers. He placed his hand on the side of her head to deepen the kiss. She squeezed her legs together as the aching between her legs started.

He broke away from the kiss to look into her eyes. "You taste like trouble."

She smiled and leaned up to continue their make-out session. Kit's tongue poked against her lips, demanding entrance. She opened her mouth, allowing him to explore. Her nipples hardened against her t-shirt, making her hyperaware of her breasts against the cotton shirt.

"Fuck that feels good," he groaned as she rubbed a hand over his sweatpants, feeling the outline of him. His dick matched the size of his body, large and thick. She leaned back until her back hit the mattress. He followed her movement, hovering over her. He trailed kisses down her neck, causing her entire body to heat up. Fuck, his lips were like small electrical currents against her skin, sending sparks straight to her core. She spread her legs, and he took the opportunity to move in between them. His hard cock rubbed against her sex, and she wanted nothing more than to get these clothes off. As if reading her mind, he pulled at the bottom of her shirt. She sat up to haul it over her head. His eyes roamed over her tits before he bent his head down and took one nipple into his mouth.

She moaned as he swirled his tongue around the sensitive area.

"Keep going," she begged.

It had been so long since a man touched her, she could get off just by Kit stroking her nipples. The coolness of his tongue ring sent chills over her body. After working on one, he moved to the next nipple. Lifting her hips up, she tried to gain some kind of friction between them. Losing her patience, she pushed at his sweatpants. Her body craved his skin against hers. He sat up and she watched in amazement as he removed his shirt, exposing his perfectly sculpted body. He had abs for days. It looked like a six-pack, but it could have been eight. He smiled that cocky grin at her as he got off the bed to drop his pants.

Her eyes bulged at his size. Fuck, he was huge. This was going to hurt. It had been so long since she had sex, she was basically a virgin. He grabbed her sleep shorts and tugged them off her legs before throwing them on the floor. Instinctually, she closed her legs, trying to hide herself. But he wasn't having any of that. He placed his hands on her knees and spread her open. She was utterly exposed. Her juices were dripping onto the sheet, but instead of feeling self-conscious, she felt perfectly safe with Kit.

"You're beautiful," he breathed as his eyes moved from her tits down to her sex. Instead of climbing on top of her, he lowered to his knees at the end of the bed.

"What--"

Her words cut short as he grabbed her hips and pulled her to the end of the bed. Without warning, he buried his face in-between her legs. Her hands flew to his hair to grab on as his tongue licked a clean line down her slit. Her back arched off the bed. She never had someone go down on her, but she couldn't imagine anyone else could make her feel this good. Her body felt like it was going to explode any minute.

"Kit. Oh, God, yes."

His tongue was relentless as he sucked and licked every inch. Her legs shook on both sides of his head as her body tingled with the threat of an orgasm.

He pulled away from her body. "Ask me if you can come," he demanded.

"Kit--"

He raised an eyebrow at her.

"Please," she moaned. She was so close. If he would just give her a few more seconds...

"Please, what?"

"Can I come?" she snapped.

He smiled before lowering his head back down. "You can come," he said against her sex before nibbling on her clit.

She let out a scream as her body vibrated, and she was finally pushed over the edge. Her hearing was momentarily lost as she tried to catch her breath. Kit moved his way up her body and lined his cock up with her entrance.

"Shit, I don't have a condom," he said.

"I'm clean and on birth control," she assured him, her voice coming out breathless.

He seemed to be thinking for a second before he nodded.

She was too caught up in the most powerful orgasm she ever had to worry about his size. But as soon as he entered her, she was completely full.

He groaned as he filled her to the hilt. Both of their bodies were covered with sweat.

"You feel so good, baby."

She hooked her legs around his waist while he relentlessly pounded into her. His balls slapped against her ass. His stomach rubbed against her clit, adding to the orgasm that she hadn't come down from yet. The headboard hit against the wall, but she could barely hear it in her daze--the room filled with the scent of her arousal.

"Fuck!" he groaned before emptying herself inside of her.

They stayed like that for a moment, both catching their breaths. Once they'd both come down from their high, Kit focused his blue eyes on her.

His lips twisted in a smile. "Again?"

She nodded. "Again."

*****

"Thirsty?"

Cam jumped at the sound of Jen's voice.

"You scared the shit out of me," she whispered in the dark kitchen. She turned the faucet off and set her glass down before facing Jen. "What are you doing up?"

Jen opened the fridge. "As if anyone could sleep with you two going at it."

Her cheeks heated up. Was she that loud?

"Don't be embarrassed. It's better than the buzz from your vibrator."

"Shut up. There is no way you could hear

that."

Jen raised an eyebrow at her but didn't say anything. Jen grabbed a piece of cold pizza out of the fridge and took a bite.

"So, is he any good?" Jen asked, her eyes zeroing in on Kit's shirt that Cam had thrown on over her pajama shorts.

"Oh my god, I don't ask you about Hugo."

"You can, and I'd tell you how big his--"

"Okay, that's enough." Cam shoved her fingers in her ears, not wanting to think about Hugo and Jen's sex life.

Jen laughed and took another bite of pizza. "Fine, but are things getting serious between you two?"

Cam pulled her fingers from her ears and let them hang at her side. "Yeah, I think so."

They hadn't talked about it, but after tonight, nothing more needed to be said.

Jen smiled. "I'm glad you got someone to clean out the cobwebs."

Cam flipped her the bird before walking out of the kitchen and back to the bedroom.

*****

"Are you sure about this?" she asked him, for what felt like the hundredth time. "This is going to be on your skin forever."

"Nothing lasts forever," he said beside her in the truck.

"Tattoos do."

She fiddled with her sketch pad as they got

closer to the tattoo shop. Kit didn't even want to look at the drawing. When she'd told him she had finished the tattoo, he'd simply said, "Alright, let's go to the shop."

"Are you sure you don't want to see it?"

He pulled the truck up to a store with big windows on the front. Namaste Ink. The store name was written in window painting with big colorful letters that looked like graffiti. Whoever owned the store was at least talented. Why didn't Kit just have the person at the shop draw his tattoo? He turned off the truck and rested a hand on her thigh. The feel of his touch sent flutters of butterflies to her stomach. After their first night together, Kit had been staying at the house pretty often. He fixed the air conditioner last week, so they didn't have to sleep with the box fan on anymore. He still hadn't returned her truck yet, and she got the feeling that he liked driving her around.

"Stop stressing out. I trust you."

Her heart melted at his words.

"And if it's bad, I can always get a cover-up," he continued.

She slapped his arm and laughed. "Come on, let's go."

The door let out a chime as they opened it. Kit held the door so she could walk in first. A familiar man sat behind the counter.

"What's up you guys?"

"Ace, how's it going?" Kit slapped his hand.

Ace--that was his name. She was getting pretty good at learning all their names, but sometimes, it still slipped her mind.

"Good. Slow day, but I'm good. Getting matching tattoos?"

She let out a laugh. There was no way she was getting under a tattoo gun anytime soon.

"Just me," Kit said.

Cam pulled the notebook from under her arm and set it down on the counter. Kit looked away as she showed Ace the drawing.

"Oh shit, this is good," he said.

"Thanks. I've never really drawn a tattoo before, so if there's anything you need to change--"

"Nope!" Kit interrupted. "I want exactly what she's drawn.'

Ace rolled his eyes before focusing back on her. "How do you put up with him?"

She laughed. "One day at a time."

"Alright, well, let me copy this and get the station ready."

He took the notebook away to a back office area. Kit grabbed her hand, and they each sat in one of the green waiting chairs. They were the only people in the shop. One of the walls was filled with basic drawings--roses, butterflies, skulls, etc. The faint scent of cleaning supplies and rubbing alcohol hung in the air.

"Are you nervous?" she asked Kit.

"No, after so many tattoos, you almost become immune to it. Sometimes, it's like I crave some new ink."

"Does that mean you're planning on covering the rest of your body?" She couldn't imagine him covered head to toe with tattoos.

He shook his head. "No. I'm just filling in any empty spots where I already have something going on."

"I'm ready for you," Ace called from another area of the shop.

She followed Kit as he walked through an archway that opened up to a few different stalls. Ace must have a couple other people that work with him because she could see that the other stations held family pictures and other personal items.

Kit sat down in the black, leather chair at Ace's station. He had the colors lined up and his tattoo gun sat beside them. She sat on a small chair in the corner of his station and watched him work. Ace shaved Kit's arms and rubbed it down with an alcohol pad. She watched in amazement as he stuck the outline on Kit's clean skin. Even though it was only a purple outline of the image, she could already tell it would come out great.

"Are you sure you don't want to see the placement before we get started?" Ace asked Kit.

He nodded. "I'm good."

Ace got to work, bringing her artwork to life on Kit's arm. He used a perfect mix of reds and oranges to make the tiger and lioness look vibrant. Kit didn't even flinch. He mostly kept his eyes closed and let his head hang over the back of the chair, as if the noise of the tattoo gun and the needle going through his skin didn't bother him in the slightest. Two hours later and Ace gave a final wipe of Kit's skin. The tiger looked better than it had on paper. The two scars down the length of the tiger's body were red and fierce. The lioness had one an angry scar down her face. The part that drew her attention was the lioness whose head rested on top of the tiger'--two different animals. Different scars on their bodies, but they stood strong with each other.

"Alright, you're all done. You want to see before I wrap it up?" Ace asked.

Kit stood from the chair and walked over to the mirror. She held her breath as he got a look. He didn't say anything for a minute.

She opened her mouth to explain but lost her courage and closed it again. What if he hated it?

"It's us?" he asked.

She nodded. His lips lifted into a smile.

"I'm the scarred tiger."

She nodded again.

"I think this is the best tattoo I have."

She let out a sigh of relief. "Thank god."

CHAPTER FOURTEEN

Cam

"You know we haven't officially been on a date?" she asked him as he put the truck in park in front of her house.

"You want to go tomorrow?"

"Oh, I didn't mean like we had to." She was perfectly happy hanging out, like what they'd been doing. She didn't need to be wined or dined like other girls might want.

"Why not? What time are you done at the bar tomorrow?"

"I open, so I'll probably be done around seven."

He smiled. "Alright, I'll pick you up at seven."

He grabbed the door handle, ready to get out, but she grabbed his arm.

"Wait, I'm going to be tired, so can we keep it low-key?"

The thought of sitting in an uncomfortable outfit while they ate dinner in the city didn't really appeal to her. Especially after getting off work.

"I can do low-key."

*****

Kit picked her up from the bar at 7 o'clock sharp. She'd been at the bar since 10 a.m., but she snuck away to use the bar bathroom to straighten her hair and apply makeup. She quickly realized she needed to buy new makeup since her eye-shadow was so old it was starting to smell like a crayon.

Kit eyes widened as she got into the pickup truck.

"Hey there," he said.

She didn't miss the way his eyes dipped to her low cut top before moving to her tanned thighs. The weather was finally starting to cool down but it was still too hot for pants.

"Hey yourself."

"You dressed up for someone?" he asked, a playfulness to his tone.

She shrugged. "That depends."

"Depends on what?"

"How well this date goes."

He smirked before pulling the truck away from the curb. "I have to run by my apartment really fast."

"The one your sister is staying at?" she asked.

He nodded. "Yeah. I have to pick up a few things for the clubhouse."

She sat back in the seat as he drove. The scent of his woodsy cologne relaxed her, and they stayed in comfortable silence until he pulled up to the apartment complex.

"Come on," he said as he turned off the truck.

She hesitated. "You want me to meet your sister?"

His sister was his only family member besides his dad, who was in prison. What if his sister didn't like her?

"She'll be ecstatic to see me with a girl."

That put her a little bit more at ease. He got out of the truck and she followed behind him up the stairs until they came to a stop at a black apartment door. Kit unlocked the door and walked in first.

"Megan," he called. She stepped in behind him and closed the door. "She's probably out. Feel free to look around. I just have to grab a few things."

He disappeared and she looked around the small, one-bedroom apartment. It was a pretty standard bachelor pad with minimum furniture but a massive TV. The place was clean--probably due to his sister.

"Fuck!" Kit's voice echoed through the apartment.

Cam ran toward the sound, stopping in her tracks as she saw a dark-haired woman passed out on the bathroom floor. Kit crouched down next to her and shook her.

"Megan!" he yelled before checking her pulse.

Cam grabbed her phone from her back pocket and called 911.

"Nine-one-one. What's your location?" the operator asked.

She looked over at Kit. "What's the address?"

"Three forty-one Pick Street," Kit said.

She repeated the address to the operator.

"What's your emergency?"

"Um, my friend's sister passed out and--"

"She overdosed," Kit interrupted. He stood up and went to the sink and cupped his hands under the water. Once he had enough, he threw it on his sister's face in an attempt to shock her back awake. When nothing happened, he slammed his fist into the wall.

CHAPTER FIFTEEN

<u>Kit</u>

They wheeled Megan down a long hallway and through a set of double doors. He was utterly useless as he stood there, staring at the closed doors. Cam tugged on his arm. In the chaos of finding Megan, he'd almost forgotten she was there.

Kit followed her to the waiting area where they sat in a couple of old, cushioned, red chairs. He'd believed Megan. She'd looked so much better than the last time he'd seen her. His hands formed fists as he thought about it. How long had she been shooting up? Had she been hooked on drugs this whole time? Was it their argument that sent her over the edge? Cam placed a hand on his knee that he hadn't realized he'd been bouncing. He looked at her concerned face, and ran a hand over his face.

"I'm sorry..." he started.

"Don't be." She scooted closer to him and rubbed a hand down his arm. "She'll be okay."

He wanted to believe that, but he didn't know. Megan still had a heartbeat when the ambulance got to the apartment, but it was faint. Who knows how much shit she'd pushed into her veins. He should have told her 'no' when she wanted to come back. Coming back to the same places can be triggering for a drug addict. He'd known that, but he still allowed her to stay in his apartment. Like an enabler; he'd given her everything she'd needed to keep using drugs. Had she even really gone to rehab, or was everything she told him a lie?

"Has she done this before?" Cam asked quietly.

"One other time in Goldbeach. She said she overdosed in California too." He shook his head. "You'd think coming that close to death so many times would make her stop."

The whole situation was fucked up, and it only proved to him that he honestly had nothing to offer to Cam. He didn't have money or the resources to give her a better life, so why was even trying? Cam would probably finish college and move to the city to work in her field anyways.

"You should probably go," he told her. "It might be a while before I hear any news."

"I want to stay."

He sat back in the chair and waited as Cam laid her head on his shoulder.

The clock ticked by slowly, and there wasn't any word from the doctor. No news was good news, right? If Megan was dead, they would have told him right away, wouldn't they? Eventually, Cam fell asleep with her head resting on his shoulder. His phone vibrated, and he managed to maneuver it out of his pocket without waking her.

"Hello," he answered, not bothering to look at the screen.

"You need to come to the clubhouse," Zeke said, his voice full of panic.

"I can't. I'm at the hospital."

"At the hospital?" Zeke asked.

"Megan overdosed," he explained.

"Oh, shit, is she okay?"

"I don't know yet; we haven't heard anything."

"Cam's with you?"

"Yeah."

Zeke sighed. "Venom is here."

His muscles tensed. Fuck, of course, Venom would show up at the clubhouse while Kit was stuck at the hospital. He needed to be at the clubhouse, but he also needed to be here in case Megan needed him.

"I'll try my best," he said before hanging up.

Cam woke up and rubbed the sleep out of her eyes. "What was that about?" she asked.

He considered lying to her, but what did it matter anyway? Their lives were one big mess, and he couldn't hide that. If this wasn't an example of how fucked up their lives were, then what was? "Venom is at the clubhouse... I need to be there."

She put a hand over her mouth. "Why is he there?"

"I don't know."

A dark-haired man in a lab coat walked out of the double doors that they'd rolled Megan through not too long ago. He approached them, and Kit stood up to shake the doctor's hand.

"Are you Megan's family?" he asked.

"Yes, I'm her brother."

"We were able to pump her stomach and get her stabilized. She's going to be okay."

He let out a breath he didn't realize he'd been holding since he found Megan lying on that floor.

"Can I see her?" he asked.

"Right this way."

The doctor started to lead him. "I'll be back," he told Cam before following the doctor.

They walked through the double doors and around a couple of corners before getting to Megan's room. Machines were hooked up to her. She didn't have one of those tubes down her throat like last time she'd overdosed. Her eyes were open, but they were heavy with exhaustion. Seeing his little sister like this was enough to make him shed a tear. The doctor left him alone with her, and he walked over to the bed.

"I'm sorry,' she croaked out.

He pulled up the chair to her bedside.

"Why?" he asked. A simple word, but it held so many more questions.

"A man..." she took a deep breath. "I was coming out of work at the gas station--that's where I got my job. A man was standing there, like he was waiting for me. He talked to me for a little bit, and he seemed like a nice guy, but then he offered me Smack." Tears rolled down her face as she tried to finish the story. "I told him that I was clean, and I didn't have any money. He basically forced the bag into my hand. Didn't charge me for it or anything. Gave me a syringe too and then took off. It was the first time I'd seen Smack in months. I was going to go straight home and flush it...but I couldn't do it." Her hand shook as she covered her face. "I'm so sorry, Kit. I tried so hard this time."

Her words were like a punch to his gut. She didn't blame anyone for her mistake except for herself. That meant a lot coming from her.

"What did he look like?" he asked her. The club would help Kit take care of this guy. Who the fuck would give out free heroin? Especially in a place like Goldbeach, where everyone was struggling as much as the next person. The man was dead.

"I barely remember--"

"Bullshit."

She looked down at her lap. "Dark hair, skinny, and tall with a crooked nose. That's all I remember."

He got up from the chair.

"Kit, please."

He walked out of the room, unable to hear her beg him to let this go. Whoever this guy was, he'd fed drugs to his little sister. Kit wasn't just going to brush that off.

Cam stood up when he reached the waiting room.

"Is she okay?" she asked.

He nodded. "Do you think you can ask Jen to give you a ride back?"

"Yeah. I figured you'd want to stay here overnight anyways." She tilted her head. "You're staying tonight, aren't you?"

"Maybe, but I have to take care of something first."

"What do you mean by 'something'?" she asked, her eyes wide.

"I got to go."

He turned around and walked away from her before she could ask any questions. On his drive to the clubhouse, he racked his brain, trying to think of anyone that fit Megan's description. Goldbeach wasn't a huge town, so there was a chance he'd run into this guy at some point. When he pulled up to the clubhouse, he knew something was wrong because everyone was there--even the guys who never took advantage of the rooms at the clubhouse.

He maneuvered his truck into an empty spot and walked inside. The bar was empty, which meant they were in the meeting room. He followed the sound of voices to the back of the clubhouse. He opened the meeting room door to reveal a pissed-off looking Gunner seated at the head of the table. The conversation stopped once Kit walked in.

Gunner's eyes flickered to him, and Gunner tilted his head towards an empty seat. Too hyped up to sit down, he leaned against the wood-paneled wall. That's when he noticed the man who looked completely out of place. It took a moment for his brain to catch up to what he was seeing. Skinny, tall, black hair, and a crooked nose.

"What the fuck is he doing here?!" Kit roared before lunging across the table.

Hugo grabbed him first, holding him back so the man was just out of Kit's grasp.

"He gave Megan the drugs tonight!" he yelled, thrashing against Hugo. "Might as well have put it in her arm!"

All he could see was red as the man's lips twisted into a faint smile. Gunner's gaze switched from Kit to the man.

"Venom?" Gunner asked through clenched teeth.

Venom. That's who pushed those drugs into his sister's hands. The man that's been threatening Cam for money. Venom was the center of all the fucked up shit happening in his life.

Venom's mouth twitched. "I might have been busy tonight."

"What the fuck is he doing here, and why is he alive?" Kit asked, no longer trying to escape out of Hugo's arms. Venom was in their territory after all.

"I came to make a deal," Venom said.

"And why the fuck would we make a deal with you?" Zeke growled.

"Why shouldn't we kill you right now?" Gunner asked.

"Because I have a man in my organization who is far too eager to take over, and if I die, he will. That man is too ambitious for his own good. If you think I'm bad, he's a monster. He's been trying to convince me to get into sex trafficking for years. Girls like your sister"--his eyes flickered to Kit--"would all be too easy to sell on the black market."

Kit fought against Hugo's hold again, but Hugo was too strong.

"What do you want?" Gunner asked.

Was Gunner really about to make a deal with this son of a bitch? His sister was in the hospital right now because of this piece of shit.

"I want my money," Venom said, his eyes turning dark. "Sell the bar and give me what I'm owed, and I'll make sure this area stays free of any sex trafficking."

"That's not up to us," Otis said.

"No? You can offer protection to a bar but not sell it and give me the money I'm owed? I thought you could figure it out."

A heavy silence filled the room.

"We'll need to vote," Gunner said.

Venom stood up from the chair. "I'll be around in a few days for your answer."

He walked past Kit to get to the door. It wasn't until they heard his car start-up that Hugo let him go.

"What the fuck was that?!" he yelled.

"Kit, I know you're mad, but we have to make this decision just like every other decision: we vote. If we kill him, we're putting everyone at risk."

Zeke snorted. "Yeah, if what he's saying is true..."

"Do you wanna take that risk?" Gunner snapped. He took a deep breath. "We have a simple solution here. We need to convince Cam to sell the bar and it solves all our problems. If we don't, we might have a bigger problem on our hands."

Kit crossed his arms over his chest. He couldn't believe they were talking about this. No one in the room spoke, everyone lost in thought.

"Those in favor of taking the deal?" Gunner asked.

Kit kept his arms tightly folded in front of him as he watched his brothers raise their hands. Gunner raised the gavel, but before he could slam it on the table, Kit stormed out of the room, slamming the door behind him.

CHAPTER SIXTEEN

Cam

She should have immediately called Jen to pick her up, but something stronger pulled her down the hall to the room that the receptionist said Megan was in. Cam's heart ached for the woman she didn't know but had seen laying on the floor in probably one of her worst moments.

She listened at the other side of the door for a noise. What if she was sleeping? If she was asleep, then Cam would just leave and call Jen. This was a stupid idea anyway. Taking a deep breath, she knocked on the door.

"Come in," a voice called from inside.

She pushed the door open to see Megan propped up in the hospital bed. Machines surrounded her, beeping softly. Megan raised an eyebrow at Cam in confusion.

"I'm sorry to barge in... I was with Kit when he, uh, found you."

She shook her head. "God, can this get any more embarrassing?"

"I just wanted to make sure you were okay. Kit told me to go home, but…"

She smiled an inch. "Yeah, I'm okay. Just fucking mad at myself."

Cam nodded, unsure what else to say. "Well, I should get--"

"Wait, are you dating my brother?" Megan asked.

"Kind of, tonight was our first date."

Kit and she had never had an official talk about their relationship status, but he did have a tattoo on his body that represented them.

Megan smiled a genuine smile. "Finally, he's dating someone and not messing around with those club sluts."

"The girls at the clubhouse?"

Megan nodded. "I haven't been around for long, but I know the younger guys at the club can be wild."

"Did you use to hang out at the clubhouse a lot?"

"Pffft--no, I can't stand the Savage Spades."

Cam didn't ask for an explanation because she didn't want to get her angry while she was still recovering.

"They're going to let me out in a day or so. I'll have to find a group or go to some kind of treatment, but I would like to meet the woman that is making my brother finally settle down. Maybe he'll even stop fighting."

"Fighting?" Cam asked.

She arched an eyebrow. “Yeah, you know, the fighting ring. He can make some good money if he wins, but it’s not worth him getting concussions.”

“Like street fighting?” Cam asked.

Megan frowned but didn't say anything. How could she not have known about this? He hadn’t had any bruises on his body in a while. She’d almost forgotten about the marks on his face when he first started coming around the bar. She should have pushed for more information. Fighting for money was stupid no matter how good you were; if someone hit him the wrong way, he could be dead. What else about Kit’s life did Cam not know about? They barely knew each other if she thought about it.

Cam forced a small smile. “I should let you rest.”

Megan nodded in agreement, and Cam walked out of the hospital room. She walked outside to the concrete stairs and sat down on the top step. Jen picked up on the second ring.

“Hey, where are you?” Jen asked.

“Um... I’m at the hospital. I was going to see if you could pick me up?” she asked, thrown off by how Jen answered the phone.

“Amire, watch the bar. I have to pick up Cam. I’ll be right there.”

“What's going on?” Cam asked.

“I’ll tell you when I get there.” She hung up before Cam could ask any more questions. This night was just getting better and better.

*****

She slid into Jen's beat up Honda. "So, what's going on?" she asked.

Jen pulled away from the curb and drove back towards town. "Hugo said Venom showed up at the clubhouse."

"Kit told me. Is that where he went?"

"I don't know, but they had a vote...and..."

"What Jen? Spit it out!"

Jen let out a sigh. "They made a deal with Venom that they'd convince you to sell the bar and give the profits to Venom. He said if they didn't agree, he'd bring his sex trafficking business into Goldbeach."

Cam's blood started to boil. She'd been calm all night, but her composure was slipping. "They can't decide what I do with my bar. I'm not selling." She crossed her arms over her chest and stared at the window. Who did they think they were? First, they barged into her bar and claimed they're protecting her, and now, they believe they can make decisions for her? Did Kit agree to this?

"Come on, Cam," Jen said.

"Come on *what*? It's my bar. If I decide to sell or not is my decision. Not some club that decided they like to drink there."

"The bar isn't making any money, and it never has. If people want to drink, they either do it at home or go into the city."

She looked at Jen in shock. Jen had never

given her opinion on Cam's business.

"I'm sorry, but Venom is a scary guy, and keeping the bar is playing with fire," Jen told her.

She hated that Jen was right. Even knowing that selling the bar would leave her without a job, Jen was encouraging her to do it. Her dad wouldn't have wanted her in this situation, but getting rid of the bar was easier said than done.

Cam swallowed the lump in her throat. "I'll think about it."

Jen dropped her off at home and then went back to the bar to close. Her shoulders finally dropped from being around her ears all day when she walked into the empty house. Who knew a first date would turn out so crazy.

*****

She'd called Kit five times, each one going to voicemail. She had class in a few minutes, but she was more worried about where Kit was. He was probably pissed after the whole Megan situation, but she needed to know where he was. Had he really agreed that making her sell the bar was the solution? If he wanted her to sell the bar this whole time, why hadn't he talked to her?

She dressed for class with no idea how to get there. She hated to wake up Jen since she'd closed last night, but at this point, she was out of options. She knocked on Jen's door.

"Huh?" Jen croaked out from the other side.

"Can I borrow your car? I have class, and Kit's not answering."

"Keys are on the table," she said.

"Thank you. I owe you one."

She grabbed Jen's keys and walked outside only to stop in her tracks when she saw Big Blue parked in front of the house. She left Jen's keys on the entry table before closing the door and walked up to her truck.

So he had time to fix her vehicle and drop it off but not enough time to answer the phone? What time was he here last night? He might be going through a lot right now, but that didn't mean he could shut her out. Even Jen knew more about what was going on than she did. Cam got in the truck, finding the keys in the ignition. Good thing the truck didn't get stolen. Did Kit even think about that when he dropped it off?

*****

She sat through a boring, hour-long lecture. It was a waste of time considering all she could think about was Kit and the future of her bar. This was precisely why she didn't want that damn club involved in her life. She needed to be focused on school. If she would have just paid Venom his monthly payment, this could have been avoided. Instead, she let herself believe for a second that a motorcycle club would take care of it. That's what she gets for relying on someone else. How many times did she have to learn that she's the only person she can depend on?

The professor dismissed class, and she walked out of the lecture hall with the rest of her classmates. There were two homework assignments that she had to get through and a paper to write if she didn't want to fall behind, but she barely had time to breathe, let alone do homework. She checked her phone to see that Kit still hadn't called her back. There were only a few places that he'd be. She started the truck and drove to the clubhouse.

His truck sat in the first spot in front of the bar entrance. She took the place next to him and threw Big Blue in park. She took a deep breath, trying to calm the fire that was in her belly. Had he really voted that he would convince her to sell her bar? He must have, or why else would he be avoiding her? When she walked inside, Zeke was sitting at the bar.

"Oh, hey, Cam." He looked around as if searching for someone. "Has Kit talked to you?" he asked.

She sighed. "No, but Jen has." She crossed her arms over her chest and raised an eyebrow.

Zeke shook his head. "I'm sorry, Cam."

"Doesn't matter. It's not up to y'all what I do with the bar anyways"

His eyes widened. "You're not going to sell it?"

"I don't know, but if I do or don't, that will be my decision."

"Cam--"

"Where's Kit?" she asked, not giving a fuck what else Zeke had to say about her business.

"Haven't heard from him since he stormed out last night. You can check his room."

She looked around, trying to figure out where his room might be.

"Down the hall, follow the set of stairs. It's the third door on the left," Zeke said.

"Thanks."

As she followed Zeke's instructions, she realized just how many rooms were in the clubhouse. There must be a room for every member and then some. When she got to Kit's door, she took a deep breath before knocking. No answer. She knocked again. Nothing. Fuck it, she opened the door herself. He couldn't avoid her forever. His body was spread out sideways on the bed. He wore the same outfit as last night. His pants now had grease marks on them, probably from working on her car. She kicked the side of the mattress.

"Kit."

He groaned in response.

"Where the hell have you been all night? I've been calling you."

If anything, he should have been at the hospital with his sister, not working in his shop. He turned over to his back. His cheek had a ugly bruise as well as dried blood crusted under his nose. Megan's words replayed in her head: *He can make some good money if he wins, but it's not worth him getting concussions.*

"Did you fight last night?" she asked.

He sat up and rubbed a hand over his face.

She snorted. "You know what, forget it."

Why did she even care? He was the one shutting her out. She had her bar to worry about. It was a waste of time coming here. She was stupid to think something serious was going on between them. He was probably just trying to be friendly by fixing her truck and inviting her on the camping trip. He said it was his and Zeke's job to make sure she was okay. That's probably all it was. She walked towards the door.

"Cam," he said so quietly she barely heard him, but she walked away anyways, shutting the door behind her.

CHAPTER SEVENTEEN

Kit

Fuck, his body hurts. The smell of Cam's perfume lingered in the room. After the meeting, he had to find a way to get out his frustration, so he'd gone to the fighting ring. Of course, he got his ass kicked because he couldn't think clearly. His mind was filled with the image of Megan lying on that bathroom floor.

After leaving the ring, he was still too hyped up to sleep, so he worked in the shop, getting as many cars done as possible. It was only once his body had been completely exhausted, and he'd dropped off Cam's truck that he finally passed out. He needed to get his ass up to the hospital to meet Megan. They'd probably release her today. If not to go home, they'd send her to a rehabilitation place.

He peeled off his dirty clothes, leaving them on the floor before getting in the shower. He let the warm water wash over him. His mind cleared the longer he stayed under the water. As much as he wanted to kill Venom with his bare hands, the club was right. Their best option was to get him out of their hair and wipe their hands clean of this. But that didn't solve the most significant problem on his hands. Megan. She needed to go back to rehab, but it's not like he had the money to send her anywhere. Maybe if he would have won some fights last night, he'd have something to offer. Getting out of the shower, he changed into jeans and a t-shirt before walking out of the room. He passed Zeke on the way outside to his bike.

"Hey, did Cam find you?" he asked.

Kit ran a hand through his hair. "Yeah, she found me."

Zeke's eyes went to the bruise on his face. "You win?"

He shook his head.

Zeke sighed. "How's Megan doing?"

"She was okay last night. I was just going to the hospital to check on her."

"Let her know that we're here if--"

"You know how she feels about the Spades."

"Yeah, I know...you want me to talk to Cam?" Zeke offered.

Having Zeke talk to Cam about selling the bar would take one thing off his plate, but that's a conversation he needed to have with her, no matter how much he was dreading it.

"She said she might not sell."

"I'm sure she did," Kit said, a hint of a smile on his face. In addition to him leaving her at the hospital last night and not answering his phone, he was sure that's part of the reason she was so pissed at him this morning. God, he really fucked up. "I'll talk to her," Kit told Zeke before patting him on the shoulder and walking out the door.

*****

"And you don't remember anything specific about the man?" a police officer asked Megan as Kit came into the room.

Fuck, he should have known the police would be involved. The officer looked up at Kit. But he wasn't just a police officer. It was the fucking Sheriff. Sheriff Garrett, the asshole who had been after the Savage Spades for years.

"Kit Wolke, what a nice surprise," Garrett said.

Kit walked towards the hospital bed and crossed his arms over his chest. "Don't mind me, go ahead and finish interrogating my sister while she's lying in a hospital bed."

Garrett's jaw twitched. "Watch yourself, boy."

"Or what?" he challenged. It was stupid to poke a bear, especially when Garrett was already sniffing too close to the club.

Garett closed his small notepad and placed it in his pocket. "You know, you're right, Mr. Wolke. There is another case I could be working on. Such as Dustin Connor, who was found in his bar...burnt to a crisp."

"I heard. That's unfortunate, although I did

hear he had a thing for young girls, so maybe it's not that unfortunate," Kit said, keeping his expression stoic.

Garrett furrowed his eyebrows, attempting to stare Kit down. He wasn't worried. If they had any evidence tying the Spades to Dustin's burned-down bar, they would have already arrested them. These crooked cops were the reason the Spades had to take things into their own hands anyways. If they had kept Dustin in custody, he wouldn't have had to die.

Garrett looked back over at Megan, who stayed quiet during their conversation. "If you remember anything, please let me know."

Megan nodded. "I will."

Garrett walked past Kit, making sure to shoulder check him. Kit gritted his teeth at the pain that shot through this arm. Fuck, he shouldn't have gone to the ring last night.

He turned his attention back to Megan. "Let's get you out of here."

*****

"Are you sure you're going to be okay here?" he asked Megan.

They'd released her from the hospital, but he felt odd leaving her alone in this apartment. Everything about it was the same but something had changed.

"I'll be fine. I found a group online. They have a meeting tonight. I'm going to go" She sat on the couch, crossed-legged.

He nodded. "Are you sure you don't need to go back to rehab?"

It all seemed too normal that she could just join a group and go to meetings after such a big relapse. He wanted to offer her more.

"I'm fine."

He nodded and tucked his hands into his jean pocket. "Zeke wanted me to tell you that the Spades are here if you need them."

She snorted.

"What is your problem with them?" he asked, finally voicing the question that had been bothering him for years. Now wasn't the best time to bring it up, but it was starting to bug him. "You need people right now. You told me that you came back here for a support system."

"Those people are not a support system. You want to know why I can't stand that club of yours?" she snapped.

"Please, enlighten me."

"Because you had them. While I was at home cleaning up after our drunk father, you were busy trying to work your way into that club. I was the one who had to clean up the mess at home." She crossed her arms over her chest as her voice broke with her admission. "You should have been there, but you weren't. You were surprised when Dad got arrested, but I wasn't because I've watched him basically try to drink himself to death. I knew it was only a matter of time."

Her words were like a punch straight to his

gut. It was so long ago that his memory was fuzzy. He'd found the club months before his dad had gone to jail when he was just a teenager himself. He hadn't thought about what Megan was dealing with at home. Kit had found a place that accepted him and he'd been too busy doing everything he could to stay in that spot. By the time their dad had been put away, he'd been spending every waking hour at the club.

"Megan--"

She put a hand up to stop him. "I don't want to get into this tonight...please."

He wanted to push her, but she was in a fragile state right now. But wasn't she always? Megan was always one step away from falling into another bender. Instead of leaving, he took a deep breath and joined her on the couch. She inched away from him.

"I'm sorry. I didn't know Dad's drinking had gotten that bad. I found a place that accepted me, and I was just trying to make the best of it. If I had known, I would have been there."

She stayed silent. The only sound in the apartment was the air conditioning running.

"In treatment, they encourage us to make amends. I never have," she admitted.

He waited for her to continue. He made a mistake all those years ago, but Megan had hurt him too. All the lying and stealing was hard to look past.

"I'm sorry for everything. I've been so mad

at you for so long. I came back because I don't have anybody else, Kit. When we were little, it was just you and me, and then you joined the club, and Dad got sick, and I was just so mad at the world and everyone."

He wrapped an arm around his little sister as she cried. He stayed quiet as she let herself feel all the emotions. After a while, she wiped her face and smiled at him.

"I'm sorry," she said.

"I'm sorry, too."

"Can we start over? I just want to put all this behind us. I want my brother back."

"I never left," he reassured her. Even when she'd been in California, he'd always worried about her.

"So, where are you going now?" she asked him.

"Well, now that you're okay, I have something else I need to deal with."

"Cam?" she asked

He raised an eyebrow at her.

"We might have talked at the hospital. I like her...a lot. Don't screw it up."

He swallowed. "I'm trying not to."

CHAPTER EIGHTEEN

Cam

She knew it was him before turning around. Her regulars were already sitting in their spots, and Zeke hadn't shown up this morning. She figured the whole babysitting thing was over now that they knew what Venom wanted. She wiped a towel over the wet glass, feeling his eyes at her back.

"Can we talk?" he asked, his voice heavy. Ignoring him, she placed the dry glass down and picked up another.

"Cam?"

The way he said her name brought a heaviness to her chest. She was stupid to think there might have been the potential for something more with him. The sound of the barstool scraping across the floor finally made her turn around and face him. His hand was on the back of the stool he'd pulled out but hadn't sat down yet.

"You're going to ignore me?" Kit asked

Ernie sipped his beer and watched the two

of them.

"Like the way you ignored me when I called you five times? Or when I showed up in your bedroom and tried to talk to you?"

She set the glass in her hand down and walked away, trying her best not to cause a scene in front of her customers. His heavy footsteps followed behind her. She got to the office and tried to close the door in his face, only for him to put a hand on the wood and stopped it from closing.

"I fucked up. I was just messed up after everything that happened with Megan--"

"Did you agree to convince me to sell the bar?" she snapped.

He swallowed, and his eyes dropped to the floor. That's the only confirmation she needed.

"Well, so that you know, I'm not selling. And you can tell the rest of your club that."

His jaw ticked. "Cam, this is serious, you need--"

"I don't need to do anything! How about you go back to your fighting buddies if you're that mad about what I do with my bar? That's where you go when things get hard, right? I was fine before you guys came in and decided to make this your new drinking spot, and I will be fine afterward."

"Fine?" he snapped. She couldn't help being happy that she finally got under his skin like he had been getting under hers. "You owed a debt to a man that wouldn't hesitate to kill you."

"News flash, nothing has changed. I'm in the

same spot I was in before."

He put his hands up in front of him. "You know what? Fine. You want to put your head in the sand and act like you never need anyone's help. Well, I'm not going to be there when it bites you in the ass."

She watched his back as he walked away. With a heavy sigh, she lowered herself into the office chair and allowed the tears to come. The lump in her throat became bigger the longer she sat there. After a moment, she wiped her eyes and stood up. Just like any other time in her life, she had to be strong and get through the day, even when she felt like complete shit.

*****

Two Weeks Later

Beep. Beep. Beep.

She searched the bed for her phone and swiped to turn it off. Her head was killing her, and it had nothing to do with drinking. She was up most of the night, trying to play catch-up on all her homework that she'd fallen behind on. She hadn't gotten home from the bar until one a.m., and she wasn't even sure how many hours she'd been doing homework.

Her body ached as she forced herself out of the comfort of her bed. And into the shower before getting dressed in a haze. Putting one foot in front of another felt like a challenge when she was this exhausted, but she did it anyway, so she could get some coffee in her system. She jumped as she came around the corner and saw Jen awake and sitting at the table.

"Shit, you scared me. Why are you up so early?" Cam asked as she walked to the coffee pot and grabbed the Folgers out of the cabinet.

"I just go home. After I got off, I hung out at the clubhouse with Hugo. I ended up staying the night."

Cam wanted to ask about Kit, but she shoved that thought to the back of her mind and pressed the on button so the coffee could brew. She leaned against the counter and watched as Jen scrolled through her phone.

"I have my early class today, so I'll be at the bar for the rest of the day if you need me."

She didn't know why she was telling Jen that. Jen knew where to find her. An uncomfortable silence hung between them. Cam already knew how Jen felt about the bar situation. She had expressed to Cam nearly every day since their last conversation that the bar was losing money.

"Kit asked about you," Jen said.

Cam's ears perked up. "What did he say?" She hated that she sounded so desperate.

"He just asked how you were doing... I wasn't sure what to tell him."

"Tell him I'm doing fine."

"Cam--"

"I'm fine, Jen. I've been fine without the stupid motorcycle club. I'm doing what I've always done. I go to school, and I run my bar."

"The bar isn't making any money, and you're exhausted!" Jen snapped.

Cam ignored her and walked out of the kitchen, forgetting about the coffee. She'd have to buy a soda on the way. The summer heat was finally starting to die down into fall weather, but she barely noticed the cool breeze against her bare arms as she walked outside. She hopped in her truck and slammed the door.

Once inside the stillness of the cab, she put her hands up to her face. She could do this. She did this last year, and she was fine. *Except that she almost failed all her classes and the bar never made money*, a little voice said in her head.

She took a deep breath, trying to calm herself. For a brief second, she wished life came as natural to her as it did Jen. Jen never had anything to worry about. She made her money bartending, paid her bills, and blew the rest on clothes or now dates with Hugo. Cam could barely even imagine a life without one hundred things on her plate. She started the truck and headed to school. Because unlike Jen, Cam had a lot on her shoulders.

CHAPTER NINETEEN

Kit

"Come on, let me help you out tonight. You look stressed," one of the club sluts cooed.

Yeah, he was stressed. He hated the way things ended between him and Cam. After being sent to voicemail so many times, he had stopped calling. He'd shown up at the bar like an idiot.

"I said I'm fine," he said to the woman who sat close enough to him that her bare legs were probably stuck to his jeans.

She pushed her tits together so he could get a view of her cleavage. But he felt nothing. The smell of her perfume was overwhelming when he was used to the faint scent of Cam's strawberry shampoo. He didn't want to look at or touch any other woman. He wanted Cam, but she was stubborn. She didn't want to face reality, but she was going to have to, whether she liked it or not. If she didn't sell the bar, Venom was going to come after her. She thought she was tough, but she couldn't handle everything by herself.

"What's wrong? Got something on your mind?" the woman asked.

He didn't even know her name. He was trying to be nice, but he was losing his patience. "Go bother someone else."

The woman huffed and stomped away.

"Kit!" Gunner called from the bar. "We got Church."

As if Kit didn't already know that. That's why he was sitting at the bar instead of underneath a car at the shop where he wanted to be.

With a sigh, he slid out of the booth and followed behind Gunner to the meeting room. He closed the door behind him since it looked like everyone was already there. He took the empty seat beside Zeke.

"You look like shit," Zeke told him.

"Thanks," he grumbled. He felt like shit too. He never thought he'd be the kind of guy broken up over a girl, but Cam had changed something in him. He missed her feisty attitude and the feel of her soft skin against his. She wasn't like anyone he'd ever been with. She was curvy and funny and had no hesitation calling him out on his shit. He hadn't been to the fighting rink since he and Cam broke things off. He couldn't deny that her words had some influence on him: *That's where you go when things get hard, right?*

She wasn't wrong. That's where he'd been letting all her frustration out for years, ever since his dad's drinking had gotten worse. Maybe his new outlet needed to be dealing with all the fucked-up shit instead of running from it. Damn, he was pussy-whipped.

"Alright, let's get started," Gunner said at the front of the room. The chattering stopped.

"Lily wanted me to remind everyone that we are required to be at the school charity event this weekend."

Groans filled the room. Lily organized all the charity work they did for the year. Part of being in the Savage Spades was doing good for the people of the town. But that didn't mean they'd choose to spend the day at an elementary school instead of...well, anywhere else.

"Can't we just donate money?" Otis asked.

Gunner shook his head. "Nope, we need to be there on bikes and help collect the donations. On another note, where are we with the bar?"

Gunner turned his attention to Kit.

He sat up straighter in his seat. "She won't sell," he said.

"She doesn't have a choice," Ace said.

"Yes, she does," Kit gritted out. If Cam didn't want their help, there wasn't anything he could do.

Gunner's eyes softened as he looked over Kit, as if taking in his overgrown beard and dark circles under his eyes. "Talk to her."

If she'd answer her phone, he would have been talking to her. Kit nodded his head, deciding not to argue. At the end of the day, Gunner was his President. Despite Kit's disagreement with the decision the majority had decided, that was the rule. If he didn't hold the level of respect he did for the club, he might have gone out and taken care of Venom himself, but the club had done a lot for him. He had to return the gesture, even if that meant stalking Cam until she talked to him.

Gunner continued talking about news happening around the town and their upcoming ride. Kit tuned him out. It wasn't until the gavel hit the table and his brothers started to leave that he was pulled from his trance.

"You want me to go with you to talk to Cam?" Zeke asked.

Kit shook his head. If she felt bombarded, she would lash out.

"Can I offer some advice?"

He didn't have anything else to lose. "Shoot."

"Make the decision easy on her. She has a lot to lose."

"How am I supposed to do that? I have nothing to offer her."

"You're wrong. You gave Megan a lot when she came here. I know you don't think it's a lot, but it is. She had nowhere to go, and you gave her a place to live and a support system. You gave her the opportunity to find a job and get back on her feet. That's not a small thing, and you can do the same for Cam if you think about it. She doesn't want to sell the bar because after it's gone, she has nothing. Give her something to run to."

He stared at Zeke, as if he'd grown two heads. Zeke patted him on the shoulder as he stood. "You'll figure it out."

*****

Kit parked his bike in the empty spot up front and took a deep breath. Convincing her to sell the bar was a challenge he wasn't sure if he was up for. Especially because he had no idea why she was still hanging on to the place. He ran a hand over his beard before climbing off the bike and crossed the sidewalk. The door creaked as he opened it.

Her green eyes met his before she quickly looked down again at her notebook. Yeah, this wasn't going to be easy. The entire place was empty. Not even the regulars were here today.

"Where is everyone?" he asked her as he approached the bar. He didn't bother sitting down.

"Ernie's in the hospital. His daughter called. Apparently, he had a bad fall last night. According to the gossip, Melinda and her husband are trying to save their marriage again. She'll be back next month."

"So, now, you don't even have your regulars?" he challenged.

She shoved the notebook away and stood to her full height before crossing her arms over her chest. It made her tits look bigger as she pushed them up with her arms. She didn't wear a touch of makeup, but she was still the most beautiful woman he'd ever seen. She didn't have to try so hard like the girls at the clubhouse. Cam, when she first woke up, looked better than all of those women put together. God, what he'd give to have her waking up next to him again...

"Did you just come here to argue?" she asked, pulling him from his thoughts.

"No, I came here to talk to you. Talk to me for once. Give me a reason why you are holding onto this place that is costing you money and stress. This bar is killing you, and it's not giving you anything in return!" He tried to keep the bite out of his voice, but he wasn't successful.

She looked away from him. A beat of silence passed.

"Talk to me, baby," he begged.

She faced him again; her eyes tearing up.

"He's here, Kit. His scent is in the walls. His favorite songs are bookmarked on the jukebox. Every time I pour a customer a drink, I think about how he laughed at me as I attempted to make my first cocktail. I know I need to sell the bar, but that's easier said than done."

He walked behind the bar and pulled her close to his chest. Her tears stained his t-shirt as she let it all out. Her body shook as the tears fell freely. She hiccuped, as if trying to get herself under control, but it was like a broken faucet overflowing the sink. Finally, she gave up and her muscles relaxed under his hold. He was helpless. All he could do was hold her as she sobbed out months of stress and grief. Kit rubbed her back as she let herself feel everything she had tried so hard to avoid. It felt like hours before she was able to breathe normally. She pulled back from him, but he didn't let her go.

"I'm sorry... I shouldn't have pushed," he said.

She shook her head. "It's not that. I know I need to sell. I've known for a while. It's inevitable. My dad couldn't keep this bar afloat, and neither can I. What am I going to do? I don't know how to do anything besides run this bar and go to school. How am I supposed to make money?"

"Move in with me?" he blurted out. He'd been thinking about what Zeke had said, and he wanted nothing more than to have Cam live with him. To wake up with her in his arms every morning. He wanted to find a way to make her life more comfortable, and getting rid of the overhead of rent would give her one last thing to worry about.

Her eyes widened. "Are you sure? That's a big step."

"I know, but I want to help. Megan is still living at my apartment for the next few months, but until then, you can stay at the clubhouse with me."

She seemed to be thinking it over. "What about Jen?" she asked.

He shrugged. "Talk to her. Who knows, maybe she'll move Hugo in."

She laughed. "I don't know about that." She

took a deep breath. "So we're doing this? I'm putting the bar up for sale and moving in with you?"

He nodded.

"What am I supposed to do for money?"

"How about you help me at the car shop on the weekends?" he suggested.

"I don't know anything about cars."

"Then you can deal with the horrible customers."

She laughed but then got quiet again.

"Tell me what you're thinking," he said.

"I can't do this if you're going to keep fighting. That's a deal breaker for me. You can get hurt, and if we're going to make this relationship work, I need you around for a long time."

"No more fighting, I promise."

She raised an eyebrow at him, like she didn't believe him. "So what are you going to do when you're mad or frustrated or anything?"

He smiled. "I guess I'll have to find another way to get my energy out." He squeezed her ass.

She laughed. "I'm okay with that."

"Are you feeling a little frustrated now?" she asked.

He gripped her ass before he lifted her onto the bar and settled between her legs. He ran a hand over her exposed leg. Fuck, he missed her soft skin. Two weeks was way too long to be away from her. His dick strained against her pants, as if begging to be let out.

"I missed you," she said before pressing her

lips to his. Her scent filled his nose, and it was like coming back home. This is where he belonged: with Cam. Wherever she was, that was where he needed to be. He tangled his hand into her dark strands before gripping tight to pull her neck back. She let out a gasp, and he moved his lips from her mouth to her neck. He gripped her thighs, and her legs spread further apart like she was begging him to get closer. He trailed kisses down her chest until he got to her cleavage. He let go of her hair, so she could lift the shirt over her head. She unhooked her black bra. He watched as her perfect tits were exposed. Her nipples were hard and begging to be sucked. Her hands ran over his shoulders then down his back where she tugged at his shirt. He took a step back to quickly undress while she took off her shorts, so she sat on the bar completely naked. God, she was the most gorgeous woman he had ever seen. Every curve was made specifically for him to run his hands over.

"What if someone comes in?" she asked, looking at the door.

He smirked. "Then I guess they'll get a show."

"Kit--"

Her words were cut off as he rubbed her clit.

"Fuck." He couldn't drag this out any longer he needed her now. It had been two, long weeks without her. He lifted her up and slid her down onto his shaft. Her body vibrated as he entered her. He was instantly surrounded by her warmth.

"Fuck, I can't..."

Her legs shook as her pussy clamped around him. He waited until she came down from her orgasm before he started to fuck her hard. Her slickness poured down his dick to his balls. It wasn't long before his spine started to tingle, and he emptied himself inside her.

CHAPTER TWENTY

Cam

Cam placed the last bottle of liquor in the cardboard box and taped it up. Hugo, Kit, and Zeke would be here tomorrow to pick up all the boxes.

The sun was starting to set, and a stream of light from the window highlighted the dust particles in the air. The real estate agent would be putting the 'for sale' sign on the front window tomorrow. She could have waited until the day the bar sold to shut everything down, but there was no reason to stay open. As Kit said, this bar had taken everything from her and gave nothing back in return.

She ran a hand over the bar top, feeling the smooth wood under her palm. This had been her life for the last few years. The place where she built a relationship with her father. The place where she cried and screamed and met her best friend.

Amire wasn't surprised that she was closing down. He found another job at Helen's the same day. She'd been scared to tell Jen because Jen had been pushing so hard for her to sell the bar anyways. Cam thought she might pull an 'I told you so,' but Jen was happy for her. A tear slid down Cam's cheek as she walked towards the big, old wooden door that she had walked through nearly every day for years.

There was so much waiting for her on the other side of this door. She could finish her degree and finally have the time to think about what she wanted to do with it. She could focus on her relationship with Kit and Jen and her new family. At least, that's what Kit told her.

He said she was now a part of the Savage Spades. She wasn't sure how she felt about that, but it was comforting to know she had so many people cheering her on. Taking a deep breath, she pushed on the door to walk outside. It didn't budge. That's weird. She tried again this time harder. Nothing.

"What the--"

That's when she smelled it. The overwhelming scene of burning wood. *Fuck, fuck, fuck.*

She rammed her shoulder into the door over and over again. This couldn't be happening. It's over. She turned around to see smoke coming from the kitchen. This was a setup. Venom. She screamed at the top of her lungs, hoping that someone could hear her. But her screams turned into coughs as the smoke got stronger.

If the liquor caught fire, she would be done

in minutes. Her body weakened, but she used the last of her strength to walk over to the window and hit it as hard as she could. Her arms felt like jelly as she slammed her fist against the glass. And then everything went black.

CHAPTER TWENTY -ONE

Kit

The smell of smoke filled the cab, and his heart hammered in his chest. Something was wrong. He came to the bar to help Cam finish up any last-minute packing, but his stomach twisted into knots as he turned the corner and saw the smoke coming from the bar. Shit!.

He threw the truck in park and sprinted toward the building. The black and gray smoke billowed out of the roof. Sirens sounded in the distance like alarm bells. He didn't give himself time to think as he slammed his body against the wooden door. It didn't move an inch. He looked down to see a metal chain wrapped around the door handle and secured to a hook placed in the concrete. There's no way she could have gotten out.

"Watch out, the firemen are coming," someone yelled to him, but he didn't care to see who it was. Cam was in there, and he wasn't going to wait around.

He looked through the window. It was so dark he could barely see anything. A loose brick lay on the sidewalk, and he picked it up before slamming it against the glass. The window shattered, falling into pieces all around him.

A cloud of smoke hit him in the face. The smoke was getting worse in the small amount of time since he'd gotten there. Once the flames hit the alcohol, it would be a done deal. He pulled his shirt over his nose and mouth, getting ready to step through the window when a thought occurred to him: *What if Cam wasn't in there? What if Venom already took her...or worse?*

He couldn't think like that. He took a deep breath of clean air before stepping through the window. His eyes burned from the smoke, but he forced himself to keep them open. She was on the ground, not far from the window. Her hair spread out over the wooden floor that looked more like char than wood at this point. Her face held a softness to it, as if she was just taking a quick nap. Fuck. She was limp and hot against his skin as he picked her up. Damn, he should have taken the chain off the door first so he could go that way. The only option now was the window.

"Hold on, baby," he told her. He stepped one leg through the window. The shards of glass rubbed against his jeans.

"Hold on; hold on," a voice said.

Kit looked up to see two firefighters rushing towards him. "Take her," he said, turning his body so they could grab Cam out his arms. He watched one of them run with Cam in his arms back to the waiting ambulance.

"Is there anyone else inside?" the other firefighter asked Kit as he helped him out of the window.

Kit shook his head. "I don't think so." He stumbled on his feet, but the firefighter grabbed his arm to keep him steady.

Everything that came next was a blur. Kit rode to the hospital with Cam in the back of the ambulance. The EMTs assured him that she would be fine, but she was still unconscious when they got to the hospital. It wasn't until she was in a room, hooked up to oxygen, and a bunch of other machines, did her eyes finally crack open. He let out a breath he'd been holding ever since he smelled the smoke. Thank god she was okay. If he hadn't gotten there in time...

She opened her mouth to talk, but her face twisted in pain. The doctor said her throat would hurt for a while.

"*Shh*, don't say anything. Do you want water?" he asked her.

She nodded, and he grabbed the water off the bedside table. She removed her oxygen mask and took a sip from the straw. She scrunched her nose as the cold water must have hit her raw throat. The door opened, and Jen barged into the room, Hugo not far behind her. Jen's eyes were wide and panicked. He had texted Zeke in the ambulance, so he must have told everyone.

"Oh my god, you're okay," she said to Cam, coming to her bedside. Cam nodded, and Jen looked over at him. "What happened? Why can't she talk?"

"The bar was set on fire," Kit said through clenched teeth, allowing himself to finally feel the anger that had been buried underneath his concern for Cam. This was no accident. Venom wanted to kill his girl. "She was unconscious when I got there. She inhaled a lot of smoke, so her throat is pretty raw."

A tear slid down Cam's cheek as she listened to him talk. He used his thumb to wipe it away. She opened her mouth to say something but then stopped, as if remembering she can't talk. Jen noticed and searched the bedside table until she found a notebook and pen. She handed it to Cam.

She wrote: *The front door was locked.*

"Someone wrapped a metal chain around it," he told Jen.

"Oh my god, who..." Jen trailed off as she realized who would do something like this.

The same person they should have killed when Venom pretty much injected his sister with heroin.

"Kit..." Hugo warned, getting a look at the rage on his face.

"I gotta go," he said, and started to walk away, but Cam wrapped her fingers around his arm. He can't stay here and do nothing, so he prayed she wasn't going to ask him too. Venom needed to pay for everything he'd done. He tried to ruin his life twice now. Cam used her other hand to write on the notepad:

You better come back home.

He leaned down and kissed her on the forehead. "I promise."

*****

The entire club was in the waiting room. They took up almost all the chairs.

"Is she okay?" Lily asked.

He nodded. "She's fine. She can't talk right now, but she's awake, and the doctor said she'd be fine."

"Thank god."

He looked over at Gunner. His face was unreadable.

"I'm going," Kit told him. He wasn't letting Venom get away with this, not after today. Damn the consequences. For all they knew, everything Venom told them about the sex trafficking ring was a lie.

"We need--"

"I'm not voting. I'm going with or without the club. So, if you're with me, I'm leaving now."

"Hold on, let's be smart about this," Gunned reasoned.

Kit shook his head. "No, he has to die."

Gunner looked around at the rest of the club. Zeke nodded his head in support, Otis nodded next, then Ace. All the way down the line, each person nodded.

"Alright, let's go."

*****

It wasn't hard to find Venom. All they had to do was drive into the city and talk to the people on the corner. For a drug lord, he wasn't very good at keeping his location secret. They pulled up to the building where Venom's penthouse was located. Kit was in his truck and everyone else on bikes.

There was no way they were getting inside there. They stuck out like a sore thumb. The couple of people who walked past their line of motorcycles stared at the bikes like they've never seen one before. It was dark outside now, so the foot traffic had slowed down a lot.

"What's the plan?" Gunner asked. He'd pulled his bike up next to Kit's window so they could talk.

"We're going to have to wait until he comes out." The bottom floor was all windows. Kit could see straight through to a lobby area and a receptionist's desk.

"That could be a while."

Kit shrugged. "You don't have to stay. I'll wait."

Gunner shook his head. "What are you going to do once we have him?"

"Kill him."

"Are you sure about that?"

"Why wouldn't I be? Cam could be dead right now because that son of a bitch couldn't wait until she sold the bar to get the money that she didn't even owe to him." He gritted his teeth as he thought about Cam lying in the hospital bed right now. He should be next to her, but he wasn't going to be able to relax until Venom was out of their lives permanently. He needed to be killed for what he did to Megan too. Everyone in town had suffered one way or another from the drugs that Venom and his men sold.

"That's a lot to have on your conscious," Gunner warned.

"There he is!" Hugo yelled.

Kit jumped out of the truck, almost hitting Gunner with the door. Hugo got to Venom first. Venom was no match for Hugo's size. He tried to fight, but Hugo easily wrestled him to the ground and put his hands behind his back, as if arresting him.

"Get the fuck off me! You stupid motherfuckers are going to regret this!" Venom threatened.

"Where do you want him?" Hugo asked Kit.

He looked up and down the street to make sure there weren't any witnesses. "In my truck."

Hugo forced Venom to a standing position and started walking him to the truck. Kit put a hand out to stop him.

"So what, you're going to kill me? I already told you what would happen once I'm gone. You must be a stupid--"

Kit landed a punch to his gut knocking the wind out of him. "Killing you immediately would be too kind. We have a long ride ahead of us."

CHAPTER TWENTY-TWO

Cam

"I'm going to be in this big house all by myself?" Jen asked as Cam stacked one cardboard box on top of another.

"This place is not that big," Cam said, doing a sweep of the entire place with her eyes.

Jen crossed her arms. "It still sucks."

"I'll have more time now, so I can always come over and hang out."

"Yeah, but it's not the same. I'm going to miss having my best friend down the hall."

Jen opened her arms, and Cam stepped in for a hug. She opened her mouth to say she'd see her at the bar, but she realized that wasn't a possibility anymore. It was a strange feeling to think a job she'd been working for so long was gone. A weight had been lifted from her shoulders, but she also felt a sort of emptiness. What would she do with her time? She already decided she'd start taking class full-time next semester, but until then, she had to learn to enjoy her time. She had to re-learn how to enjoy life when it wasn't filled with work and stress.

"I'm so happy for you," Jen said into her shoulder.

They pulled back, and Jen had a smile on her face. The front door swung open; Kit and Hugo walked back inside from the truck.

"How many more we got?" Kit asked. He was dressed for the move today in a muscle shirt and old jeans.

When he'd gotten back to the hospital the night the bar had burned down, he said that Venom was taken care of. She never asked for details because she knew in her heart Kit only did what he felt like he needed to do. He was protecting her and Megan from a monster.

"Just these two," she said, waving her hand at the stacked cardboard boxes. As he bent down to grab him, she couldn't help noticing the way his muscles bunched up. Every time she looked at him, she was reminded of why this was the right decision. She couldn't white-knuckle her way through life. She had to enjoy her life now with this gorgeous man. She said her last goodbye to Jen.

Once Kit strapped down all the boxes in the back of the truck, he joined her in the cab.

"So this is it," she said, looking out the windshield at the house she'd called home. She'd moved to Goldbeach to find her family: her dad. She would have never guessed her family would be a bunch of leather-cut wearing men called Savage Spades. She smiled at the irony.

Kit stretched over the console to kiss her lips. Her heartbeat quickened as his lips moved against hers. She breathed in his familiar, woodsy scent, allowing it to calm her. All the anxiety she felt during the process of talking to insurance agents and packing all her stuff to move seemed to wash away. This moment was all that mattered. She was ready to move forward. He pulled back and looked back and forward, as if searching her eyes for something.

"Are you having second thoughts?" he asked. His chest stopped moving, as if he was holding his breath as he waited for his response. She put both hands on the side of his face and leaned in for another kiss.

"Never."

Epilogue
Kit

"Are you almost done with the Toyota?" Cam called to Kit through the open door that led from the waiting area to the garage.

He grabbed a towel to wipe his greasy hands on before walking into the waiting room. "Almost," he told her.

She furrowed her eyebrows together for a moment as she looked down at the phone. She picked it up and pressed it to her ear.

"It will be ready to pick up in an hour Ms. Jenkins. Okay, we'll see you then."

She hung up the phone and wrote something down in a notebook.

"I don't know how I feel about you making my schedule," he said as he leaned against the counter. He peered over to look down her shirt. She was wearing a low cut top that gave him the perfect view of her tits. Autumn had turned into winter, and even though they were inside, the shop was freezing. She wore a heavy jacket that covered her arms but kept it unzipped.

"Well, I like to actually have customers," she said, finally looking up at him. Her green eyes widened as he caught her staring down her shirt.

"Kit!" she snapped, zipping up her jacket.

He looked behind her at the empty lobby.

"What?"

"You're like a horny teenager."

He rounded the desk and grabbed her hand

to stand with him. Then he wrapped his dirty hands around her waist and pulled her close. Her body felt warm flushed against his body. Warm would have been the last word he used to describe Cam only a few months ago, but now she was his safe spot. The place where he could tell all his problems.

She was still going to school full-time. The insurance money from the bar covered the rest of her tuition. She still had a year until she graduated. Megan was able to get an apartment of her own. So he and Cam had been able to move out of the clubhouse. He didn't mind staying there, but after a few weeks, he'd noticed Cam's annoyance with the club sluts. He thought he would miss staying at the clubhouse, but he was enjoying giving himself some distance.

Cam made the apartment a home. It was filled with decoration and candles. There was no better feeling than getting off work and coming home to her sitting on the couch in one of his t-shirts with a textbook open on the coffee table.

When he hired her to work at the front desk at the shop, he didn't think it would have such a significant impact. Due to the better customer service, he had more people from town bringing in their cars. Which meant Kit couldn't work whenever he wanted to. Cam made sure that the shop had precise working hours. "I want you home at night," she'd told him, and on the day she posted the hours on the window.

"You smell so good," he said against her neck. Goosebumps ran over her skin.

"Like a lioness?" she teased.

He laughed. "Yes, just like my little lioness."

I hope you enjoyed reading *Savage Spades*. Please consider leaving a review of this book on either Amazon or Goodreads. Reviews mean the world to self-published authors.

About the Author

K. D. Clark is a United States author living in Saint Louis, Missouri, with her high school sweetheart and being a dog mom to two amazing pit bulls. She spends every minute she can either working on her books or reading the great works of other romance authors. For more information on book releases and her writing process, please feel free to check out her website, Instagram, Facebook, and Twitter.

Website

https://kdclark926116107.wordpress.com/

Twitter

https://twitter.com/KDClark2

Instagram

https://www.instagram.com/authork.dclark/

Facebook

https://www.facebook.com/AuthorKDClark/

Sneak Peek of Twisted Judgement

About the book

Alpha male Giovanni Marino takes center stage in the new mafia romance ; Twisted Judgement.

Giovanni is a man born into
the world of darkness.
Nothing in New York City happens
without him knowing about it.
He is used to people fearing him
and meeting all his demands.
He's sure this won't be any different.

In a moment of desperation Ave
turns to the lesser of two evils.
A man she hopes will feel obligated to
keep her safe because of her father.

After years of trying to distance herself from the criminal underworld she finds herself right back in it.

This book can be read as a standalone

Chapter One

Wes

His hand connected with a stack of DVDs, letting them fall to the floor as he strolled down the aisle. "How many times we gotta come out here, Diego?" James said, his voice echoing from the front of the store. Wes couldn't see them over the shelves but he knew James was laying it on him thick. The movie store was failing. Of course it was, people didn't go rent movies anymore when they could get all the movies they wanted right on their couch. If he thought about it hard enough he felt bad for Diego's family. Two young girls who after a few months were probably going to be without a father. *But that's what happens when you make a bad deal with bad people who you can't pay back.* At the end of the aisle sat a large gumball machine. The red base held a spot where kids could insert two quarters. Some of the gumballs were chipped, showing the white inside. The machine and the candy inside were probably older than him. Wes pressed his hand against the glass and pushed it over. The movie shelves shook

from the impact. The glass immediately shattered, leaving pieces all over the old carpeted floors. It was loud enough that he was sure that Diego's family, who lived above the movie store, would have heard.
"I'll get you your money...I...I...promise," the man stuttered, trying to save his own life but even he had to know his days were numbered. This was the second time they'd been to the store. They hadn't left with any money last time. Wes doubted they'd leave with any today. Tommy, his boss, was getting impatient with the old man. The glass crunched under Wes' black shoes as he moved down another aisle knocking everything off the shelves. It was going to take days for the old man to clean up the store.
"That's what you said last time now isn't it?" James asked. The pictures on the wall shook as James must have slammed Diego against the wall. Wes rounded the corner. Diego had his eyes slammed shut as James fisted his t-shirt and held him against the yellowing wall.
"Please...I mean it this time...no games," the man begged.
James looked over at Wes.
"What do you think, Wes? You think we should whack him right here?"
His question was all for show. They couldn't very much whack him without getting the go-ahead

from Tommy but Wes went along with it.

He shrugged. "It would save us a third trip."

"Wait, wait. Here." The man dug in his pocket. His wrinkled hand shook as he grabbed some crinkled bills and offered it to James. "Please, this is all I have."

James turned to Wes, and he nodded. James let go of the man's shirt and snatched the money out of his hand.

"It's not going to be pretty next time we gotta come here, Diego," James threatened as they walked out of the store and onto the busy New York street.

The sun was out today but it didn't keep away the chilly wind temperatures of the autumn air.

"How many more we got?" James asked as they walked to Wes' car. James was dressed in a pair of jeans and a t-shirt. He was probably planning on going to the shop after they were done here.

"Two more. The strip club on 8th and that old office building."

He got into his black Nissan Maxima. He'd left his motorcycle at home today since he'd known James would be riding along with him. His phone vibrated with a text.

Are you still coming by tonight?

"I know what that look means," James

said, his eyes trained on Wes.

"Don't know what you're talking about," Wes said as he started the car and pulled into the street.

"Yeah ok."

Avé was a part of his life that he preferred to keep secret. She didn't want to be a part of this life so he tried his best not to drag her name into it. Plus the fewer people who knew about her the better. The world he lived in was dangerous and if people found your weak spots that was the first thing they went for. It was the reason he'd moved his mom and sisters out to Oregon in a small town. It was far enough away from the Cosa Nostra life that no one could find them. He had failed at protecting Willow, his youngest sister, once and he'd vowed to never let anyone in his family down again. He hadn't joined Cosa Nostra for the money or recognition, although those things were nice, he'd joined to protect his family. He'd grown up in a tough neighborhood and joining Cosa Nostra meant protection.

"You ready?" Wes asked James as he parked in front of the strip club.

James reached for the door handle. "Always."

*****

Wes maneuvered his motorcycle to the parking space next to Avé's silver Lexus. The drive from his home to Avé's apartment in the city wasn't too long but with

New York traffic on a Friday evening, it had taken him longer than anticipated. He unhooked one leg from the bike to stand on the black asphalt, removed his helmet then set it on the seat. He looked up at her brownstone apartment building. Her father must have paid a fortune for the place considering that it had its own small parking lot around back. He walked to the front door and typed in the door code on the metal pad. She'd just recently given him the code since he'd been coming by more often. When Tommy had told him he needed to keep an eye on a new girl in the city several months ago he'd thought it was a joke. But Avé's father was a legend in Cosa Nostra and he wanted to make sure his daughter was safe. Tommy assigned the job to Wes and the first time he'd laid eyes on her he couldn't have been more grateful. The door didn't so much as creak as he opened it even though the building had to be at least a hundred years old. It had been completely renovated at one point. The door opened up to a hallway with black shiny tile and crisp white wall. There were only two apartments on this level and two more on the floor above. The windy staircase was at the end of the hallway. His footsteps echoed as he approached her door and knocked. A moment later the door swung open.

She stood in front of him dressed in a tight purple skirt that hugged her hips. The skirt traveled all the way up to her small waist. She'd tucked in a white t-shirt that complimented her tanned skin. The V-neck of the shirt gave him the perfect view of the mounds of her breasts. Her nude colored lips twisted into a smile having caught him staring. This woman was the most beautiful thing he'd ever set eyes on. He'd known the minute he'd seen her that he couldn't look at other women the same. Nobody could compare. It was her doe eyes that really sucked him in. They made her look innocent like a baby deer. Her face was perfectly proportional and not a hair was out of place. Even her toes were perfectly pained as she stood barefoot in the doorway.

"Are you going to come in or do you prefer the hallway?" she joked.

He smiled and walked into her apartment. Her bare feet patted against the hardwood floor as she walked into the kitchen.

"Do you want a drink?" she asked, opening the fridge.

"No, I still have to work tonight."

He walked into the living room and kicked off his shoes before sitting down on the large sofa. Her living room itself was the size of a lot of New Yorkers' entire apartments. The place was exactly her personality. Beautiful furniture and expensive decor. Nothing was out of place. Every time he'd come over, it was spotless. She stepped around the corner with a glass of wine in hand and came to sit by him on the couch. She turned sideways so she could lay her perfectly smooth legs over his lap.

"You have plans tonight?" he asked as he trailed a hand over her leg. He wanted to stay here as long as she'd allow him to. He was so pathetic. She'd made it clear she had no interest in getting involved in something serious with a man connected to the mob. He didn't blame her but every time they spent time together he found himself wanting to stay longer and longer.

"Going out with a few co-workers," she said.

"And you're pre-gaming with wine? Lame."

She playfully shoved his shoulder.

"Shut up. I like wine."

She set the glass down and removed her legs from his lap so she could straddle him. His dick was instantly hard. He held on tight to her hips, loving the feel of her curves under his rough hands. He moved his hands down to her exposed thighs and pushed her skirt up her body. His eyes widened when he laid his eyes on her bare pussy. He imagined her at work all day in this tight skirt completely nude underneath.

"Fuck," he moaned, his dick straining against his jeans.

She lifted her t-shirt over her head and quickly unclasped her bra. Her breasts fell out hitting against her body. He ran his hands up from her thighs, to her waist, and then finally to cup both of her breasts. "You are so beautiful," he said. She wasn't one of those women that needed to hear those words but he told her anyways because it was the truth.

She smiled at him. "You aren't so bad yourself."

She leaned forward and pressed her plump lips against his. He'd have lipstick all over him after this encounter but he didn't care. As the kiss deepened, she started to move her hips against his hard cock. It wasn't long before he couldn't take it anymore and he lifted her up slightly so he could unbutton his pants. Once his jeans and boxers were slid down to his knees, he placed his hands back at her hips, guiding her down until he had completely filled her up. The warm sensation as her walls closed around him made his toes curl. Avé moaned and grabbed his shoulders to hold onto for balance, taking a moment to adjust to his size before she started to move. He grabbed her ass with both hands and squeezed. Each time she came down on him she'd grind herself against his groin. He'd had sex with a fair amount of women but none could compare to Avé. She wasn't shy or self-conscious about her body. She knew what she wanted and he was happy to give it to her. Her walls started to tighten around his dick and he knew it was only a matter of time before she came. As he glided his hands from her ass to her thighs, her legs started to shake. He thrusted up to increase their pace. His balls tightened but he held back, making sure she'd come before he did. Her breathing became shallow, he knew she was close. He let go, finding his own release just as she collapsed against his chest. He took a moment to catch his breath as Avé laid against his chest. Their sweaty bodies stuck together. Once he'd come down from the high, he realized his mistake. He was falling for a woman that would never love him back.

Made in United States
North Haven, CT
29 September 2023